New Girl

(Hardcover title: Break a Leg!)

New Girl

(Hardcover title: Break a Leg!)

by

Stella Pevsner

AN
APPLE ®
PAPERBACK

SCHOLASTIC INC.
New York Toronto London Auckland Sydney

ISBN 0-590-40103-3

Text copyright © 1969 by Stella Pevsner. Illustrations copyright © 1969 by Barbara Seuling. All rights reserved. This edition published by Scholastic Inc., 730 Broadway, New York, NY 10003, by arrangement with Crown Publishers, Inc.

12 11 10 9 8 7 6 5 4 3 2 1   5 6 7 8 9/8 0/9

Printed in U.S.A.

Contents

1

Cupcakes and Mis-er-y

FRANCES SANDERS leaned against the school with one foot propped on the bricks, waiting for Debbie to come out of their sixth-grade class. Debbie was always one of the last kids out of the room, but it wasn't her fault. She couldn't help it if she was stuck in the same row with Andrew Willis. Miss Hawley dismissed them row by row, depending on which was the quietest, and any row with Andrew Willis in it had to be the noisiest in the whole school.

A group of third-graders drifting down the street began chanting:

> "Six more days and we'll be free
> From this place of mis-er-y.
> No more pencils, no more books,
> No more teachers' dirty looks!"

Any other year, Fran would have been cheered by the verse. Today, only one word stood out . . . *mis-er-y*. And that was what the summer was going to be.

Debbie was going away to camp. Not for two weeks, or even a month, but for two whole months. And so that wiped out any chance of Fran's having a good summer.

You shouldn't count on just one friend, her mother sometimes said. But it was different with grownups. They met lots of people. Fran brushed aside the thought that there were lots of girls in school. She wasn't interested. Debbie was her best friend, and you could only have one best friend. Period.

Fran started walking toward the sidewalk. If I count to one hundred by fives, and then turn around, she'll be coming out the door, she told herself. "Twenty-five, thirty, thirty-five . . . " A station wagon was easing to a stop in front of the school. It looked exactly . . . it *was* theirs. "Mother," she called, racing to the curb, "what's the matter?"

"Nothing." Mrs. Sanders peered through the open window. "I'm on my way to the store for cake mix and thought you might like to ride along. Move over, please, Chip."

Fran's brother, who was almost eight, shifted in his seat.

"Mother," Fran said, "I can't. Debbie's coming over to help paint the puppet theatre. We want to get that part done at least, before she goes to camp."

"There's Debbie," Chip said, pointing. "Going down the street with those girls."

"She couldn't — " Fran spun around. Sure enough, Debbie was walking in the opposite direction from the way she should have been going, head bent, talking with two other sixth-graders.

"Mother," Fran coaxed, "wait just a minute?" She darted after the girls, calling.

Debbie turned around and frowned. "What is it, Frances?"

Fran stopped, shocked at the coldness in her friend's voice. "Aren't you coming over?" she stammered. "To paint the puppet theatre?"

"Oh, I forgot." Debbie glanced at her companions, embarrassed. Her face flushed as one of them said, "Puppets? Oh, no!" and giggled.

Fran could feel an answering flush on her cheeks, but she stood her ground, waiting for Debbie.

"Gee, I don't think I can," Debbie mumbled, avoiding Fran's eyes. "We're going over to Shirley's to talk about camp and all. Why don't you go ahead. . . ."

"Come on, Debbie," one of the girls said, "if you

want to be in on the plans." She started to walk away and her friend joined her.

Debbie hesitated, her eyes following the girls. "It's not as though it was a *real* theatre . . . you know, like last spring."

"We could revive that play — " Fran stopped. They couldn't do that play. Or anything. Debbie would be gone. "Oh, forget it," she murmured.

Released, Debbie hurried after her new companions. She called over her shoulder, "I'll phone you later."

Fran watched, unbelieving, as her friend walked down the street away from her, her arms linked with two other girls.

"Are you coming or not?" Chip called from the car.

Fran got in behind him. She didn't feel like talking.

"Debbie's a freak," Chip observed, sucking in his breath as he tightened the seat belt.

"Chip," Mrs. Sanders said, stopping to let children cross, "I've told you not to use such language. And for goodness' sakes, loosen that seat belt a little. You're turning blue."

"Am I?" Chip, sounding pleased, strained to see his reflection. With a sigh, he let out the belt a little.

Debbie and the girls had turned a corner and were out of sight, but Fran could still see the way Debbie had looked when the word *puppet* was mentioned.

Why was she ashamed of their puppet theatre? Debbie was even the one who had thought of it, after they gave up on the real live play.

"With a puppet show, we can make up the lines as we go along," Debbie had said. "All that matters is to have it look cute and keep lots of action going. The trouble with our real play was it was too much work."

The trouble with the real play, Fran now thought, was that it had never happened. They had planned to present it down in the Sanders' basement, and let Chip pull some old screens back and forth for curtains. One Saturday in March they had started getting together costumes. "After we scrounge up as many long skirts and high heels and wild hats as we can," Debbie had said, "we'll write a script to go with them." They had written a page or two of dialogue on the typewriter one day, but after the carbon copy turned out too smudged, they had given up and turned the play into a fashion show. "Just for the time being," Debbie said, "until we find a script somewhere." But they never had.

Mrs. Sanders drove a little faster, now that they were out of the school zone. "We're getting mix for Chip's cupcakes," she said to Fran. "He wants to take them tomorrow because school will be out when his birthday comes."

"I still get my party on June fifteenth, though, don't

I?" Chip asked. And without waiting for a reply he added, "I know what kind I want. A secret agent party."

"What's a secret agent party?" Fran asked, curious in spite of her mood.

Chip turned and poked his glasses back up on his nose. "You send out invitations in code, and for the main game you have a spy hunt with clues and all. It's real neat. You and Debbie can set it up."

Fran leaned forward. "Something like a treasure hunt, only we make a mystery." Remembering, she slumped back. "Forget it," she said, "Debbie will probably be gone by then."

"That's okay, *you* can do it."

Mrs. Sanders interrupted. "You can discuss that later," she said. "How would you like to choose some candy decorations for the cupcakes?"

"Really? Anything I want?" Chip asked, delighted.

"Anything within reason."

The minute they got into the supermarket, Chip disappeared. Fran and her mother went down the baking goods aisle.

"Oh dear," Mrs. Sanders said, eyeing the various kinds of chocolate mix. "This seems such a lazy way, but I promised him I'd bake them tonight, and I still have all those phone calls to make about the library addition. I'd better pick up some chops, too, and lettuce."

Just as they reached the check-out counter Chip rushed up, carrying a big cellophane bag. "I found 'em!" he said triumphantly.

"*Them,*" Mrs. Sanders corrected automatically, getting out the money.

"Mother!" Fran said, horrified. "You aren't going to let him put *these* on cupcakes, are you?" She held Chip's package in front of her mother. "Look . . . false teeth!"

"Aw," Chip said, grabbing the bag, "they're candy ones."

"Mother, they're weird. Everyone would think we're weird too!"

Mrs. Sanders glanced at the big clock on the wall and sighed. "Chip, couldn't you find something more suitable? Gumdrops, maybe?"

Chip scowled. "You said I could choose anything I want."

"Within reason, she said," Fran reminded him.

"Within reason means not costing too much, and these don't." Chip put the candy on the moving counter and stood guard.

"I can't see that it makes much difference," Mrs. Sanders said. "They're eaten in such a hurry."

Riding home, seeing girls walking along together, Fran forgot about false teeth and cupcakes. The word *mis-er-y* floated back into her memory. There'd be nothing to do this summer . . . nothing different to do . . . with Debbie gone. When Fran had agreed with her family, early in the spring, to stay home this summer and save for a big family vacation next year, she had never dreamed her best friend would desert her.

At the door, at home, a neat little blue sign greeted them.

DON'T RING THIS DOORBELL OR YOU'LL BE ELECTROCUTED

"Chip," Mrs. Sanders said warningly, "you know what I told you about pasting those stickers on walls."

"I didn't know you meant *outside* walls," Chip said, all innocence.

"Well, you know it now."

While her mother started the cupcakes, Fran went to her room to change.

As she was sitting on the floor, tying her sneakers, Chip came to the open door and stood stiffly. On his old T-shirt was pasted a sign, MY MOTHER CAN LICK YOUR FATHER. "Can I help you paint the puppet theatre?" he asked. "I won't smear."

"I'm not going to paint today. Maybe I won't ever. I don't care what happens to that old theatre."

Chip's face lit up. "Then can I have it?"

Fran remembered the trouble she and Debbie had had converting the old refrigerator box into a theatre . . . and the curtains they'd made, and the tiny Italian Christmas-tree lights they were going to use for footlights. Chip waited, his face almost glistening with eagerness, "I don't know about having it," Fran said, "but I guess you can paint it."

"Gee, thanks!"

She called, as he bounded down the hall, "Don't forget to spread out plenty of papers!"

When Fran went to the kitchen her mother had finished mixing the batter. Fran put the little fluted cupcake liners into the pans. "It's too bad we don't have white ones," she said. "These pinks and blues are going to look terrible with those awful false teeth. Why did they have to make the gums so orange? Ugh!"

Mrs. Sanders laughed. "I doubt that the children will notice the color scheme, but maybe we'd better leave a plain cupcake for the teacher, in case she has a weak stomach."

When the pans were in the oven, Fran decided to go see how Chip was doing.

He had spread newspapers over most of the drive-way and was squatting Indian fashion, painting one side of the theatre. The front, a bright royal blue, gleamed in the low rays of the sun. Fran squinted, wondering if that white patch was a reflection or if Chip had skipped a small place. When she got closer she saw it was a tiny sign, stuck above the opening of the stage.

"Chip!" She was suddenly furious. Why couldn't he stick his old signs on his own property! "Who said you could — " She stopped short. This wasn't one of his silly signs. Just the word *Theatre*.

Chip, painting happily away, murmured, "I thought you'd be surprised. I found it in the paper . . . here . . . by my foot." And as an afterthought, "I stuck it on with gum."

Fran glanced at the newspaper. And then she stared. What? What did it say? She dropped to her knees and read, SUMMER THEATRE PROJECT FOR KIDS.

She snatched up the paper, almost too excited to read. "Chip," she gasped, "they're going to have drama classes for kids this summer!"

"Oh, barf." Chip slapped on more paint.

"In the Park District." Fran felt the same sort of excitement which gripped her whenever she and Debbie thought of some new plan. "Imagine, real drama classes . . . not just some play in our basement!"

"Barf," Chip again commented. *Barf* meant getting sick to your stomach, like on a bus on a field trip, but Chip said it all the time, just to be annoying.

There was no point in staying around, listening to Chip. Besides, there was no time to lose. Registration, it said, closed Friday. Tomorrow!

"Mother," she called, slamming into the kitchen, "listen to this!"

"Just a second, honey, I'm listening to this," Mrs. Sanders said, indicating the portable TV on the counter. The five-minute news capsule was on.

Fran reread the article while she waited. *Climax of the course will be a series of one-act plays to be presented in the auditorium of Lincoln High School*, it said. Real live plays before an honest-to-goodness audience!

The oven bell began ringing just as the news broadcast ended with a cereal commercial. It was that girl with a wide smile saying, "Mmm — it's yummy!" For the hundredth time Fran wondered what was so special about *her*. She wasn't really pretty. Still, the smile held Fran until the commercial ended. She clicked off the set as her mother set out the cupcakes to cool.

"Now, what did you want to tell me?" Mrs. Sanders asked.

"Oh. About this." Fran handed her mother the clipping. "They're going to have drama lessons this summer, and plays at the end of them. Could I sign up?"

As Mrs. Sanders was reading, Chip came into the room and the phone rang.

"I'll get it," Fran said.

It was Debbie. Fran trailed the long cord into the dining room and sat on the floor. "Listen!" she gasped. "You'll never guess what. I may get to go to drama classes this summer, and imagine, they're going to do plays at the end of summer in the high school, on the big stage!"

"Boy, are you lucky!" There was undisguised envy in Debbie's voice. "It would have to be *this* summer, just when I have to go to camp!" Her voice changed a little as she said, "How come you didn't tell me about it before?"

"I just found out. It was in the paper. Oh, Debbie, isn't it wonderful?"

"For you, I guess. Well, I have to eat now. I just called because . . . uh . . . well, for no reason exactly."

"I'll see you tomorrow. Oh, and Debbie" — now that things were suddenly reversed, Fran found herself feeling a little sorry for her friend — "I'll try to remember everything that happens and tell you about it."

"Sure. Bring the clipping to school tomorrow, okay?"

"I will."

Fran whipped the cord around the corner and hung up the phone. She could hear her mother in the bathroom telling Chip to wash his *arms* too.

On the counter by the cupcakes row after row of white teeth grinned foolishly up at her.

Fran grinned back. It might not be such a bad summer after all.

2

New Girl in School

THE LAST DAY of school finally came, and with it a surprise announcement.

"Boys and girls," Miss Hawley said, "in a few minutes I'm going to introduce a pupil who just moved to Fairview and who will be your classmate next year."

There was a general shuffling and comments, "Who? Where?"

"When you quiet down," the teacher suggested, arms patiently folded. She looked as though she would be glad when school was over, too. "This new pupil," she continued, "comes to us all the way from California, and I'm sure you will do your best to make her feel welcome."

Her. Then it was a new *girl*. Fran was glad, but Andrew Willis wasn't, judging from the way he was clasping his middle and making gagging sounds.

"Who," Miss Hawley said, silencing the class, "can tell us how far California is from Fairview?" Hands shot up. "Yes, Richard?"

"About two thousand miles. As the crow flies."

"Let's leave the birds out of this," Miss Hawley said dryly. "Now, who can name some of the principal products from California?"

Ugh, Fran thought. A geography lesson at a time like this. She was eager to see the new girl. She was probably suntanned ... Sun-Kist ... no, that was oranges. Anyway, the girl from the Golden West would be blonde and be wearing sharp-looking clothes. Fran shivered a little in anticipation. She had never met a girl from California.

"Come now," Miss Hawley urged. "What is a principal product?"

A pause, then from the back of the room, "Disneyland!"

Miss Hawley smiled in a resigned sort of way as the class roared. For about the tenth time her eyes glanced toward the clock. She walked to the door and looked down the hall.

In a moment she called to the class, "Quiet, please,

here she comes," and went out to the corridor. Even without a room monitor, everyone was quiet. Fran could hardly bear the suspense. It was like that time at the theatre with Aunt Margaret, when the audience was hushed, waiting for the star's entrance.

The principal hovered in view for a moment and disappeared. Then Miss Hawley entered, all smiles. "Boys and girls, I would like to introduce Veronica Lindquist . . . from California."

Again, complete silence, as everyone leaned forward, craning to see.

"Veronica?" Miss Hawley urged, taking a step toward the door.

A girl entered. Without looking right or left, she walked smack to the center of the room. With one hand on her hip she turned and faced the students as though daring anyone to utter a sound.

No one did. Somehow, Fran felt, the whole room was as surprised as she was. This was no golden, sun-kissed girl. Her hair, a brownish-yellowish color, straggled limply past her shoulders. Her bangs almost concealed her eyes. The part of her eyes not hidden by hair was covered by glasses pushed down on her nose. Instead of the crisp orange or yellow cotton dress Fran had somehow expected to see, the new girl wore a gray sweatshirt with the sleeves cut off and

an old faded Peanuts picture on the front. Her short skirt was rumpled and she wore sandals.

Miss Hawley crossed to the newcomer and seemed about to touch her shoulder, but at a cold, steady look from the girl, she clasped her hands in front of her instead.

"Even though it is the last day of school" — Miss Hawley paused automatically, but for once, everyone was too dazed to cheer — "the teaching staff thought it would be nice for Veronica to meet you so you could get to know each other this summer. Especially those in her own neighborhood." Turning, she asked, "Where is it, again, that you live, dear?"

"Two-twenty-three Elmwood Lane," the girl said, looking bored.

Miss Hawley looked around questioningly. "Debbie, isn't that your street?"

"Yes, Miss Hawley. But I'm going to camp."

Several of the boys booed. Debbie tossed her head.

Miss Hawley, looking a little harassed, shifted her eyes right past Fran, forgetting that she lived in the same neighborhood. She turned once again to Veronica. "Would you like to tell us what town you come from, dear?" She had never called anyone *dear* the whole school year.

In a loud, clear voice Veronica announced, "I'm

from Hollywood." And staring straight at Debbie, she added, "The glamour capital of the world."

Debbie blinked rapidly and her mouth opened a little.

There seemed the briefest flicker of a smile on Veronica's face before her eyes swept the room.

"That's . . . uh, interesting, Veronica," Miss Hawley said, hands fluttering at her collar. She cleared her throat. "Suppose you find a vacant seat" — she indicated one near the front of the room — "while we finish clearing out books and papers." She moved briskly to her desk, and in a voice a little louder than usual announced, "Anyone with library books please bring them to me, and please see that all art supplies are returned to their proper places."

Now there was a surge of noise and activity as pupils piled books on desks, crumpled papers or shoved them into tattered folders. Fran turned to look at Debbie. Debbie, now recovered, shifted her big blue eyes in Veronica's direction and then rolled them upward in an *Isn't she awful* look.

Fran halfway returned the smile and went back to the emptying of her desk. In a moment, she stole a look at the the new girl, and a feeling of pity came over her. Sometimes people acted aloof because they were frightened or ashamed. Maybe Veronica was poor, and didn't have anything else to wear. Maybe she wore her hair all shaggy like that because . . . because. Fran couldn't think of any reason why a girl would wear her hair like that.

Veronica turned abruptly and stared at Fran. Fran smiled shyly. There was no return smile.

Feeling her cheeks flush, Fran dipped her head to look into her desk, and pretended to search for something. Who did that girl think she was, anyway? She didn't want to be friendly. She had just come to the class on the last day . . . to show off. Hollywood!

She was nowhere in sight as Debbie and Fran walked home together, arms full of school supplies. Their gym sneakers, tied by their own laces, dangled from their loaded arms.

"Did you notice her hair?" Debbie asked. "She ought to get it cut." Debbie's dark hair was long, too, but it was sleek and shiny. Fran envied it so much. She had let her own hair grow earlier in the year, but it was too wispy and curly. And so she had followed Debbie's advice and had it cut. It was just as well. Nothing she could do would make her as pretty as Debbie.

"Those bangs!" Debbie continued. "They'd drive me crazy."

"Me too," Fran agreed. "You'd suppose someone from Hollywood . . ."

"And those clothes!" Debbie interrupted. "Imagine standing up in front of the whole class in an old beat-up sweatshirt." She made a rumbling sound of disgust deep in her throat.

Umm." Fran agreed a bit quietly. The trouble was, she could imagine what it would be like to get up in front of a group looking like that. It would be terrible. And then another thought came to her. "I'll bet she didn't know the principal was going to make her come down to the room. Maybe she just went to the school to register and —"

"Dressed like that? I wouldn't even scrub the floor in such an outfit."

Fran didn't answer, but she was thinking that Debbie had probably never scrubbed a floor. Period. Even though Debbie's older sister had got married, and moved to an apartment, Debbie still didn't have to do a thing around the house.

"Oh-oh." Debbie began walking faster. "Watch out. Here comes Andrew Willis." Even among themselves, they never dared call him anything but Andrew. "Hang onto your things," Debbie said.

Both girls, clasping their belongings to their chests, walked on, waiting for Andrew to start something. Nothing happened. They glanced at each other, then turned to see what the pest was up to. Andrew was waiting for them.

He stopped and so did they. "Hello, girls," Andrew said in a high-pitched voice. "I'm Veronica Tongue-Twist. And I'm all dressed up to meet my new classmates!" He put his hand on his hip, stuck his nose in the air and posed, while Debbie gave out with the expected laughter.

"Don't you think I'm adorable?" Now he swayed back and forth.

"No, I don't!" Fran burst out, surprising herself. And now that she had taken the plunge, a whole year's anger poured forth. "I think you're a big nuisance . . . and stupid too." Her voice faltered, "To . . . to make fun of people's names. They can't help their names!"

Andrew's hand dropped from his hip and he became himself again. His worst self, with his face red and angry-looking. "Oh, Frantsy-Pantsy," he jeered. "Little goody-goody Frantsy-Pantsy."

"Stop it!" Fran yelled, knowing it would do no good, but unable to help herself. "Stop it!" She began walking rapidly away, blinking to keep back the tears. That was the worst name he had ever called her.

"Frantsy-Pantsy . . . oh, the sweet little Frantsy-Pantsy!" He said it over and over, but his voice became fainter. Fran walked even faster.

"Hey, can't you take it easy?" Debbie complained, trailing somewhere behind. "He's not following us."

Fran slowed down and Debbie fell into step beside her. "Boy, you really started something," she said.

"*I* started something!"

"You shouldn't have said anything. He'll make life miserable for you this summer. Everywhere you go, it will be Frantsy-Pantsy. Ugh. That's terrible."

"I won't be around him," Fran said. "I'll be at drama classes. And when I'm not there I'll be home. Helping Mother," she said without conviction.

"Well, thank goodness, I'll be away at camp." Debbie gave a sigh of satisfaction. "It will be one big relief to be away from that creep. Although I'll miss you," she added loyally. "Want to go shopping with Mom and me for jeans and things this afternoon?" she asked, as they were about to separate at the corner.

"I don't think so." Right now, Fran just wanted to be alone. "See you tomorrow, maybe."

As she hurried home, she remembered how her father always said people should have the courage of their convictions. "If you think something is wrong, say so," he told her. Well, she had told Andrew where he was wrong, and he'd make her pay for it.

When Fran walked up her driveway she saw that practically the whole flower bed in front of the house was filled with pansies. Her mother was planting still more.

She looked up and smiled at Fran. "Do you think

I have enough pansy-faces? I've always wanted a whole . . ." She broke off as Fran burst into tears and dashed toward the kitchen door. *Pansy-faces. Frantsy-Pantsy!*

Chip was sitting at the kitchen counter struggling to get the lid off a peanut-butter jar. "It's about time you got here," he said. "I almost starved to death. Hey." He looked at his sister in astonishment. "What's the matter with you?"

Fran turned to go, but her mother was coming through the door, towel in hand. "What in the world, Fran? What happened?"

Blocked, Fran turned and leaned on the counter by the sink, tears streaming down her cheeks.

Mrs. Sanders pulled off her gardening gloves, and put her hand on Fran's shoulder. "Did someone do something?"

Fran wiped away her tears. "It's that Andrew Willis. He called me . . . Frantsy-Pantsy! I was so humiliated!"

"In front of the whole class?" Mrs. Sanders asked.

"No. Just in front of Debbie. But next thing you know, it'll be all over the school."

"Today's the last day of school," Mrs. Sanders pointed out. "By fall he'll probably have forgotten all about it. Maybe he'll even be in another room."

"Maybe." It wasn't just the name-calling, though, Fran thought. It was a little bit of everything.

"Frantsy-Pantsy," Chip murmured softly.

"Now," Mrs. Sanders said firmly, "don't you start that, Chip. Anybody's name can be twisted around to sound silly."

"Yeah." Chip leaned his chin on his fist. "Even Willis. I think I'll call him Willy." He beamed. "Silly Willy."

Mrs. Sanders laughed, but Fran was horrified. "Don't ever do that," she warned. "He'd beat you black and blue. Why," she said to her mother, "we're not even allowed to call him Andy. It has to be Andrew, or *pow!*"

"Goodness." Mrs. Sanders took the peanut-butter jar from Chip, rapped the lid with a knife, and unscrewed the top. "What shall we do this afternoon to celebrate the fact that school is out?" she asked.

"Go shopping? For clothes?" Fran suggested, remembering Debbie's plans. Shopping would take her mind off things. Besides, she'd love to have something new for drama classes.

"You do need some clothes," Mrs. Sanders agreed. She stepped out of her gardening loafers and tossed them into the garage.

"Clothes," Chip murmured, "barf. Drama classes, double barf."

That evening at the dinner table Mr. Sanders asked about the last day of school. Fran, thinking of her two new dresses, suddenly remembered Veronica... standing in front of the room in that old skirt and sweatshirt. "We met a new girl today," she said.

"A new girl on the last day of school?" Mr. Sanders asked. "Isn't that a bit unusual?"

"They wanted her to meet the kids so she could get acquainted this summer."

"Oh? Where is she from?"

Fran looked around the table. "She's from Hollywood. Hollywood, California."

"Wow!" Chip's eyes widened behind his glasses. "Does she know any actors who play secret agents? It would be neat to have one show up for my party Sunday."

"Speaking of your party," Fran said, pushing her chair away from the table and starting to clear the dishes, "if I'm supposed to help with that secret agent game, you'd better tell me the point of it."

Chip, remembering the family bywords, *Don't walk into the kitchen empty-handed,* grabbed up his plate and followed Fran. "Simple," he said. "You plant clues and hide the prize so we can dig it up."

"What's this?" Mrs. Sanders asked, coming into the room with more dishes. "Chip, no digging any holes for tin cans in the yard, party or no party."

"Mom. . . ." Chip managed a hurt look. "You know I'd never build another miniature golf course again. Not after you almost broke a leg."

Mrs. Sanders smiled grimly. "Horses break legs. Mothers break heels off their best pumps. So whatever the game, I repeat, no digging."

"Okay," Chip agreed. "We'll have to think of something else, then. The guys are all set for something terrific. I guess they expect it to be the party of the year."

"Somehow," Mrs. Sanders said with a sigh, "I think it might be."

3

Chip's Party

Fran couldn't think of any place to hide the secret agent prize. She couldn't even decide what the surprise should be.

Her father came to her rescue.

"Why don't you make the treasure an ice cooler full of pop?" he suggested. "Remember, boys are always thinking in terms of food or drink. And what could be better than cold pop after a wild, hot chase through the neighborhood?"

Fran was hesitant. "But what's the crime?"

Mr. Sanders picked up his newspaper. "I understand Chip has invited all fourteen boys in his room. That's crime enough so far as I'm concerned."

Fran was inclined to agree. For her part, she'd like to cool them off with the garden hose. Hose . . . sprinkler. A thought came into her mind. Why not pretend that someone had swiped the sprinkler, so they'd have to cool off with pop, instead?

It wasn't an especially spine-tingling situation, but it was something to work with, at least. She'd call Debbie, and together they could make up the clues and keep the boys chasing around the neighborhood for a long time.

If only it didn't rain!

Luckily, Sunday was bright and warm. Debbie, who was due to leave for camp the next day, came over after lunch to help the Sanderses decorate the patio. They had nearly finished when the phone rang.

"I'll get it," Chip called out as he ran into the kitchen. He came back in a moment, subdued. "It's Aunt Margaret, Mother. She wants to talk to you. She sounded real worried."

Fran felt alarmed. Aunt Margaret, who was really not their aunt at all, but their mother's cousin, was not the kind to get upset over nothing.

Mrs. Sanders handed the crepe-paper streamers to Mr. Sanders. As they continued decorating, they heard murmurs of Mrs. Sanders' voice coming from the kitchen. When she came out they knew for sure something had happened.

"It's Great-Aunt Clara," she said. "She's had a bad fall and Margaret is all upset. She's called the doctor, but I feel we should run over . . . just in case. . . ."

"Of course," Mr. Sanders said. "You never know, at her age." He hesitated. "But whom can we get to oversee all this until we get back?" A light breeze rippled the red, white, and blue streamers on the patio lamp stands.

"Now, don't worry about a thing," Debbie said. "I can manage this party. With Fran's help."

"You mean —" But Fran stopped. She was so used to letting Debbie take over that she was afraid now to point out that she was the one who should be in charge. "I mean," she said instead, to her parents, "the boys will be gone most of the time."

"Even so, you never can tell. Well, one of us should be back soon. And you can call us if things get out of hand."

"We will," both girls promised.

Mr. and Mrs. Sanders must have been less than a block away when the first trouble started.

The front doorbell rang. Fran ran to answer and before she could even get the screen door open, a jet of water struck her in the face. It was Mark Harris, with a water pistol.

"My parents had to go some place, so they sent me over early," he said. "Where's Chip?"

"Around back on the patio. But you give me that water pistol," Fran said. "You aren't supposed to squirt people at parties."

"Says who?" He ran around the house and Fran darted through the dining room and kitchen and out to the patio to meet him just as he rounded the corner of the house. "Give me that gun," she repeated. She was answered by another squirt, which dampened the shoulder of her dress.

"Come on, Mark, cool it," Chip commanded. "The water fight isn't until later."

"What water fight?" Fran demanded.

Chip looked abashed. "I told the guys they could bring water pistols for later on, if things got dull. Well," he defended, noting his sister's outraged expression, "secret agents carry guns, don't they? And these are just loaded with water."

"Give it here," Fran commanded, holding out her hand toward Mark.

"Better do it," Chip advised. "Or there may be trouble."

"You can just bet on that," Fran muttered, taking the gun inside and putting it on the counter. Within fifteen minutes, there were more than a dozen plastic guns piled high.

"It isn't even two o'clock," Debbie commented.

"And they're all here already. We might as well start the game."

Fran, who was trembling a little at the wild whoops and wrestling in the yard, agreed. There was no point in calling Aunt Margaret's. Her parents wouldn't even be there yet.

They went out and tried without success to round up the boys. Several were wrestling on the lawn, two were chasing through the neighbor's backyard, and at least five were in the maple tree, judging from the way the leafy branches swished and swayed. Fran could feel perspiration on her upper lip, although it wasn't all that hot. "Hey, kids!" she called. The slip of paper with the first clue was damp where her fingers gripped it.

"Come on, you kids. *Now!*" Debbie bellowed. It was hard to believe such a dainty girl could sound so bossy.

The boys on the lawn drifted up. The others dropped from the tree and joined them.

Almost before Fran had finished explaining the game, Carl Donen snatched the first slip from her fingers and the boys were off with a great whooping and hollering.

"Boys!" Debbie groaned, as she sank onto a patio chair. "Thank goodness we don't have any around our house!"

"Maybe you will," Fran couldn't resist saying, "if your sister has a boy."

"Oh, really!" Debbie sighed dramatically. "I'm not talking about *babies*. Besides, he'd be my *nephew*."

While Fran was secretly agreeing that it might be more of an advantage to have a tiny nephew than a rowdy brother, Debbie said, with a sigh of satisfaction, "And there will be no boys at camp all summer. I can hardly wait."

Fran wondered if Debbie were really as glad as she pretended to be. And she wondered, also, if there would be any boys at drama class. Probably not. Boys didn't like acting. They just liked to act up. "Let's have a bottle of pop," she suggested.

"Okay," Debbie agreed. "I really need it to calm my nerves."

The whole bottom shelf of the refrigerator was filled with cans of pop. Cans, Mrs. Sanders had decided, were safer than glass bottles.

"Should we carry a supply out to the table now, to have them ready for the boys?" Fran asked.

"No, the patio is too hot," Debbie decided. "We'd better wait an hour."

The telephone rang. "It's all right," Fran assured her mother. "The boys are off on the hunt. It's very quiet here. Now."

When she hung up, she told Debbie that the doctor

39

said Aunt Clara's leg wasn't broken, just sprained. "He's bandaging it, and Mother says they'll be home in an hour. Thank goodness."

Fran and Debbie took their pop to a shaded area of the patio. They had taken just a few sips when one of Chip's friends, Jeff somebody, came around the bushes. He was followed by another party guest whom Fran didn't know by name, and then Mark Harris. The rest of the group, faces red and perspiring, pushed each other as they looked wildly under chairs and even cushions.

"Where is it?" "Yeah, hey, it's supposed to be here!" they yelled.

"What?" Fran asked, unable to believe her eyes.

"It says on this last clue," Carl shouted, *"So you'll have to cool off on the patio, with pop."*

Mark snatched the paper from his hands. "That's what it says," he confirmed. "Pop."

The two girls stared. "Do you mean," Fran finally stammered, "that the hunt is over?"

"Yeah." Robert Carson wiped his streaming forehead. "I thought we'd never finish."

"You didn't go every place!" Debbie accused.

"Oh, no?" Chip emptied his pockets on the redwood table. "Here are the slips. Twelve of them. We're dying of heat. Shall we go get the pop?"

"Oh, no, you don't." Fran blocked the way to the

screen door. "You all stay right here. We'll bring it out." She and Debbie slipped inside the door and latched it. "Now, behave, or you won't get any at all."

The boys, panting and cross-looking, flung themselves around the patio.

In the kitchen, Fran looked at the clock. "Only two-twenty," she gasped, looking at Debbie. "What shall we do?"

Debbie snorted. "I'd send them all home. But then, it's your problem."

Fran bit her lip. "Would you help me carry the pop out on trays? They'd fight if we just took two at a time." They loaded up, and though there were a few skirmishes about flavors, the boys were too hot to fight very long.

"What'll we do now?" they said in a matter of minutes.

Fran, wincing as the boys stood and jumped on the cans to squash them, felt a moment of panic.

"Let's eat," one of the boys suggested. This was followed by a chorus of approval.

"I don't think Mother would . . ." Fran began. But even if she called, it would be some time before her parents arrived. And in the meantime . . .

"Oh, feed them," Debbie said carelessly. "Anything."

The girls took out the ice cream in individual cartons, and cupcakes. Fran was thankful her mother had decided to save the birthday cake with candles for the family dinner. She couldn't have coped with the cake ceremony, not with this mob.

By the time the last boys were served, the first ones were looking about for something to do.

"Hey, Sanders," Mark said to Chip, "did your folks get you the Alamo game?"

Chip looked at him in surprise. "You said not to ask for it, we could use yours."

"Oh, didn't I tell you? I lost some of the parts last week. Gee, I was counting on you to get one. You really muffed it!"

The boys looked at each other angrily.

"Fight!" someone shouted.

"Naw, open the presents." Several of the guests began rummaging through the red plastic clothes basket for the gifts they had brought. "Open this one first!" "No, mine!" "Hey, Donen, you're always first!" "Yeah?"

"Oh, be quiet or clear out of here," Debbie said rudely.

"I'll get a bag for the papers," Fran said, with a worried smile. In the kitchen she noted it was now two-forty. "Mother, Dad, hurry," she murmured.

For a while, it seemed the boys were calmed down,

as they examined model kits, gyroscopes, parachute games. Then a baseball was unwrapped.

"Let's get up a game in the backyard!" John suggested.

"No!" Fran commanded. There was no telling, with windows and all.

"Then what are we supposed to do?" Chip complained. "Hey, I know!" He darted into the house and came out loaded with water pistols. "Come on, guys, choose your weapons!"

"That does it!" Debbie said. "I'm leaving."

"Oh, no!" Fran knew Debbie didn't like to get messed up or anything, but surely . . .

"I'll be back," Debbie called, already heading out across the lawn, "when those roughnecks clear out of here."

Don't bother to come back at all, Fran was tempted to call. But how could she, on this last day before Debbie left for camp?

"Choose up teams!" Chip raced back with a big plastic watering can. As Fran watched, helpless, Chip filled the can with water from the hose and set it out in the yard.

The boys crowded around the bucket, scuffling to get at the water. As soon as one boy filled his gun, he immediately emptied it into the face of a boy stooping to try to fill *his* gun.

"You boys aren't supposed to . . ." Fran shouted. A stream of water soaked her hair and ran down her face.

Fights were breaking out. Almost all the boys were dripping wet.

"Now listen," Fran yelled, knowing no one would. "You'd better calm down." The screen door slammed behind her.

"What's going on here?" Mr. Sanders demanded.

"Oh, Dad." For a moment Fran didn't know whether to laugh or cry. "They . . . they . . ." She couldn't go on.

Her father stood and surveyed the scene. What had been, one hour before, a gaily decorated patio, was now a shambles of squashed pop cans, pieces of ribbons and birthday paper, all water-soaked, scattered hunks of cake, frosting smeared on the table, and melted ice cream oozing across the flagstones.

Mr. Sanders grinned weakly. "The party of the year."

"How's Aunt Clara?"

"Calmed down. She just sprained her ankle, but Mother's staying a while. I'm glad she is. Whew." He walked out to the boys and issued a few orders, then came back to the patio. "They might as well get *completely* soaked," he said, with a smile, "so we'll have good reason to send them home. In the meantime, suppose you and I clear up this mess. Where's Debbie, by the way?"

"She . . . had to leave," Fran said.

They tossed all the rubbish into the garbage can Mr. Sanders brought around from the garage. Then they took down what was left of the decorations.

"I'll send the boys on their way now and hose off the patio," Mr. Sanders said.

Fran went inside and put on dry clothes. Then she began clearing up the kitchen. *Boys,* she thought. One of them meant trouble and a group meant catastrophe. She wouldn't care if she didn't see another boy all summer.

The front doorbell rang. Fran ran to let Debbie in.

There on the front porch, in a clean set of clothes, stood Mark Harris.

"Hi, Fran," he said, smiling angelically. "Can Chip play?"

4

First Day of Drama Class

WHEN FRAN WALKED toward the Park District for her first drama class that Monday the sky looked bluer, the grass greener, and the flowers almost dazzling. It was like a scene on a color slide, with everything brighter than life.

This was a special day. The beginning of her career in the theatre. Did people, working in their gardens, sense this? Maybe someday they'd muse, "Ah, yes, I remember the summer Francesca Von Saunders — Frances Sanders she was known as, then — made her debut. In fact, I saw her as she walked by, that very first morning. I could see right then that someday she would be a famous actress — so talented, so charming." Fran made a mental note to start being charming. To everyone except Chip, of course, who would only take advantage.

The glow lingered for two full blocks. Then it began to diminish, as though the lights were going bad. The Park District building, coming into sight as Fran rounded a corner, was the same old building, with its craft and meeting rooms, and with the pool and tennis courts and baseball diamond outside. Fran could see children in twos and threes drifting in that direction. And she was all alone.

Would there be anyone at all she knew, taking drama classes? Would she be stuck all summer with a group of strangers? Probably everyone else was taking the course with a special friend. Debbie, she thought, why did you have to desert me this summer of all summers?

Inside the long, flat building it was cool and quiet. A sign taped to the wall stated that drama classes would be in room 102.

There were five girls in the tiny auditorium, clustered near the front, talking and giggling. They barely glanced at Fran as she walked in and sat on a folding chair in the section opposite them.

At first Fran turned eagerly at the sound of each new arrival, but it was always the same. Girls in twos.

Or a girl who was welcomed by the ones already there. Never anyone Fran knew, or at least knew well enough to be singled out and greeted. She gave up and sat with her eyes facing the front.

Suddenly a voice from the rear rang out. "Lights, camera, action!" Oh no. Not Andrew Willis! But there was no mistaking that voice. And without even turning around, Fran knew from the hoots and scufflings that Andrew had his sidekick Harold with him. Good grief! Wasn't there any escape from Andrew? For a moment she thought of leaving. But the door was at the back of the room.

"Sorry I'm late."

Fran turned slightly to see a woman wearing black slacks and a white knitted top walk briskly up the center aisle and to the front of the room. She looked as though she might be a tennis coach. Only she carried a clipboard instead of a tennis racket.

She eyed the class. "I assume," she said, "you're all here for the drama sessions. If not, you'd better escape before we cast you." She made a mock smile. "I'm Miss Blandings," she said. "You can call me Roxie. We're going to be informal."

While the class took in this information, the teacher consulted her clipboard. "It looks like the same old story," she said, with another grim smile. "Two boys, ten girls. In the eighty or more people signed up for these courses, not more than ten boys. What I ought to do is throw them all together in one class. But I'm not up to it. Any questions?"

A girl waved her hand in the air.

"Just speak up," the teacher said. "We're informal."

"What play are we going to be in?" the girl asked.

"Who knows? It depends upon how well you people shape up. We'll do the plays in the high school where there will be plenty of seating room for doting relatives."

"Do I understand," a voice from behind Fran said, "that all eighty of your pupils are going to present plays?" The voice sounded strangely familiar. Fran looked around. There was Veronica Lindquist in the same old Peanuts sweatshirt, teamed this time with a pair of cut-off jeans.

"That's it," Miss Blandings said, "all eighty." Her brown eyes beneath the curly black hair looked from face to face. "That means seven one-act plays in one evening for the audience and one big headache for me. Any more questions?" She paused. "Then let's get to work. When I call your name, get up on stage. Sally Forsythe."

A girl Fran recognized as being in one of the other sixth-grade rooms at school got up and self-consciously walked up the arched steps and onto the stage. Other girls followed as their names were called. Fran knew some slightly. Others were obviously from another nearby school.

"Andrew Willie," called the teacher.

Andrew's face turned red. "Willis," he said.

"Sorry. Typographical error." Miss Blandings made the correction. "Frances Sanders." Fran walked to the opposite side of the stage from Andrew.

"Veronica Lindquist." Veronica came to stand next to Fran.

"Hi," Fran whispered. "Remember me? I'm in your room at school."

Veronica looked her over. "Hi," she said carelessly.

She doesn't want to be friendly, Fran thought. And after I went out of my way to defend her! Of course, Veronica couldn't know about that encounter with Andrew, but still, when a person tried to be nice . . .

The teacher laid her clipboard on a table and joined them on stage. "First, let's get squared away on stage directions," she said. "As you face the audience, your right is *stage right*. Point to stage right, everybody." Arms shot out to the right. "Now, stage left."

Andrew Willis, on the right end, punched Harold Holbrook, standing next to him, as he shot out his left arm. Fran saw Harold stagger as though he had been mortally wounded.

Miss Blandings ignored them. "I am standing *down-*

stage," she said. "Down, near the audience. Rita, show me where *upstage* would be."

The girl whose hair was swept back except for a curl plastered in front of each ear looked at Sally Forsythe next to her and shrugged her shoulders. They both giggled.

"Oh, for Pete's sake," Veronica muttered.

"Who can figure it out?" the teacher asked.

Veronica walked upstage, and stood with her hand on her hip, bored. The two girls scowled.

"Okay. Upstage is up, away from the audience. Harold, walk to *center stage.* Or *stage center,* as it is usually called."

Harold looked at Andrew and grinned. Then with a loose, sprawling walk, he paced to the center of the stage and stopped. "This it?" he asked, rolling his eyes.

"I can see we have great acting talent here," Miss Blandings observed. "Now, the *wings* are directly off the stage, beyond the vision of the audience. Betty, go stand in the right wing, and Claire, in the left wing. This part" — Miss Blandings walked over and touched the upright edge of the stage — "is the *proscenium* arch. Susan, stand next to the proscenium."

The teacher returned to her original place. "Now, again, what is this area called?"

"Downstage!" chorused the group.

"And you there?" she pointed to Veronica.

"Upstage!"

They went through the places, with only Veronica remembering the word *proscenium.*

As the group went back to its seats, Fran heard the teacher ask Veronica, "Have you had any stage experience?"

Veronica hesitated. "No," she said shortly. This time she sat in the chair next to Fran.

"You people in the back, move up front," Miss Blandings commanded. "I mean you, boys. Now remember," she said when they had quieted down, "when you're sitting out here, all stage directions are reversed. So later on, when you have scripts that read, *Exit stage right,* remember, it's as you face the audience."

Miss Blandings picked up her clipboard and ruffled through some pages. Fran saw, across the aisle, Harold and Andrew whispering and snickering. Then Harold nudged Andrew.

"Roxie?" Andrew called. Harold stuck his hands over his face and hunched his shoulders, shaking with laughter. Clearly, Andrew was calling the teacher "Roxie" on a dare.

"Yes?" She looked up from the clipboard.

Now both boys dissolved in laughter, their faces almost down to their knees.

"Well?" prodded the teacher.

"I just wondered, Roxie," and Andrew pulled down the corners of his mouth, trying to control his mirth, "when we're going to begin acting."

"Right now," Roxie said, laying down the clipboard. "So nice of you to volunteer. Come on up front."

Now the whole class laughed. Fran happened to glance at Veronica, and they smiled in unison. Why, Fran thought, she's not so stuck-up after all. And another thought struck her. There was something vaguely familiar about Veronica's smile.

"Come on, Willis, we're waiting," Roxie said. And when Andrew had dragged to the front of the room, she added, "We're going to loosen up today with a few pantomimes. *Pantomime*, as you probably know, means to act out a bit of business without the help of words."

Andrew shrugged. "I don't get it."

"We'll make it easy on you. Pretend you're eating a caramel. Go through the motions."

Roxie half sat on the table, hands gripping the edge. "Get going," she urged.

Andrew, ignoring the snickers of his friend Harold, nonchalantly popped an imaginary candy into his mouth, chewed vigorously, and then swallowed noisily. He then made a huge bow and started toward his seat.

"Just a minute," Roxie called.

Andrew stopped.

"Do you chew paper and all?"

Andrew smiled sheepishly as the class erupted with laughter. "I forgot."

"In a pantomime, every little action counts. Let me demonstrate." Roxie stood up. "I'm going to do a little scene and when I finish, let's see if you can trace my actions."

She began walking, holding her hands in front of her, as though gripping a pole. She walked across the room, stopped, leaned over, and appeared to take something up and lift it to her shoulder. She gave it a couple of pats and then replaced it. She turned, looked up, held out her hand, palm up, and then rushed off, still pushing the imaginary object.

Now she stood in front of the group. "All right, what was I doing?"

"Pushing a cart in the supermarket!" someone called.

The teacher raised her eyebrows. "Really? So what did I lift and put on my shoulder?"

"A sack of potatoes," Harold said.

Roxie shook her head wonderingly. "I've seen some strange sights in my day," she said, "but never anyone in the supermarket patting a sack of potatoes. Besides . . ." She held out her palm and looked upward. "What was all that about?"

"I know, I know!" Rita waved her hand wildly.

"Just say it."

"It was starting to rain!"

Rita looked triumphant as the teacher said, "Well, that came through at least."

Roxie strolled back and forth. "So we've established that I was outside, obviously, and it started to rain. But what was I pushing?"

"A lawnmower?" Andrew suggested.

Roxie shrugged. "Could be. But what about the action when I leaned over and picked up something?"

Andrew thought a minute. "You ran over a squirrel."

"Boy!" Roxie hit the heel of her hand against her forehead. "You kids are a little squirrelly yourselves." She shuddered and shook her head. "Ran over a squirrel." She sighed. "Didn't *anyone* get it?"

Fran, feeling shy in front of these strangers, half raised her hand. Then she remembered that they were supposed to speak up. "I think you were pushing a baby buggy," she said.

"Well, thank goodness. I was beginning to wonder if I was out of touch with the world. Now . . . what's your name?"

"Fran."

"Fran, can you describe my actions?"

Fran, with all eyes upon her, felt her face flush. "You were pushing the buggy, and the baby started to cry, and you picked it up and put it on your shoulder, and then it started to rain, so you went home."

"Right! Okay, people. Go home and dream up a pantomime for the next session. And don't give me anything pointless like someone ironing, or combing your hair. I want a complete story, with a beginning, a middle and an end. Okay, scram. See you Thursday. If I survive."

Fran was a bit disappointed. This wasn't acting. It was just baby make-believe that anyone could do. And there wasn't even the fun of costumes.

Instead of joining the rush from the room, Fran dawdled, hoping the boys would disappear fast. If Andrew called her that hateful name in front of this class, she'd never want to come back again. Luckily, by the time she reached the hall, the boys were whooping it up way down the street. "I wonder," she said to Veronica, who had come along beside her, "why those two signed up for drama classes."

"Their mothers probably wanted them out of the house," Veronica observed. "To my mother, now, it doesn't matter. She works all day, anyway." She took hold of a loose thread on her jeans and jerked it off.

"Aren't you lonesome?" Fran wanted to know. "I mean, by yourself all day?"

"Lonesome! I haven't the time. I'm always out and about. I have to do a lot of things and meet a lot of people and find out who I am."

"Who you are?"

"Sure. Then, someday if I decide to be an actress, I'll be able to play other people."

Who you are, Fran thought. How strange. She knew who *she* was. Fran Sanders, who lived with her family and whose best friend . . . She wondered what Debbie would say if she were here.

"Do you want to be an actress?" she asked. Veronica really wasn't pretty at all.

"That, or something else," Veronica said, with a yawn.

Fran knew she was asking a lot of questions, but she couldn't resist adding, "How come you left Hollywood?"

Veronica stretched. "My dad got transferred. Say, should we go somewhere and get a hamburger? I haven't had breakfast."

Fran stopped, shocked. "Breakfast? It's almost noon."

"Oh, well, then, call it lunch. Is there a place around here?"

"Only downtown. But I have to go home."

"Okay," Veronica said pleasantly. "Just point me in the direction and I'll find it. I never get lost."

"Start toward my house and then I'll show you."

Veronica nodded and they walked alongside the pool and to the tree-lined sidewalks.

"I can't get over all this shade," Veronica observed. "Out there it's sun-sun-sun. What do you do in the winter?"

"Why, we ice-skate and go tobogganing, and . . ."

"We do have palm trees," Veronica interrupted. "But they're kind of kooky. Have you ever been on a movie set?"

"No," Fran said, bewildered at the conversation. "Have you?"

"Sure. But now they're mostly TV studios. Alice used to work in the wardrobe department at Metro. Alice is my grandmother. But now she works in a wig factory." Veronica pushed back her bangs. "She's kind of weird, isn't she?"

"Who?" Fran asked, startled. "Your grandmother?"

"No," Veronica said impatiently. "Roxie."

"I like her," Fran heard herself saying, although to this moment, she, too, had thought their teacher a little strange.

"Oh, I like her," Veronica said. "She just isn't what I expected out in the Midwest." They had reached

Fran's corner. "I can find my way now. Sure you won't join me for a hamburger?"

"Maybe some other time," Fran said, as she turned in the direction of her house.

Veronica smiled, gave a little wave, and set off.

It was surprising that she knew her way around town in so short a time. But it looked as though Veronica was going to be a surprising girl in many ways. And again came the teasing thought that somewhere, somehow, Fran had glimpsed that smile before.

5

An Encounter with the Boys

"ALL RIGHT," Roxie said Thursday morning, laying aside her clipboard. "Who wants to be first?"

No one budged.

"You might as well volunteer and get it over with," she remarked.

Sally Forsythe strolled to the front of the room, with Rita trailing behind her.

"We worked out a pantomime together. Is that all right?" Sally asked.

"Go to it." Roxie eased herself onto the edge of the table.

That's not fair, Fran thought. She knew what she really meant was, I wish I had planned a pantomime with a partner. But then, she didn't have that close a friend.

Instead of going up on the stage, the girls went to the front of the room. Everyone shifted to get a good view.

Sally started on one side and Rita the other. They bent from the waist and with palms forward, seemed to be pushing something. Back and forth, back and forth they went. Then they stopped, and together, lightly lifted something and placed it on top of something else. Then one girl began rolling something again while the other searched through her pockets. Sally then lifted her imaginary object and placed it high over the other two. Now, as Rita made motions in the air, Fran suddenly realized the girls had been building a snowman. Rita was putting on stones for eyes, nose, and mouth.

Obviously, the light dawned all over the class. Kids began whispering to each other or shaking their heads knowingly.

"Okay, class," Roxie said, "What were they doing?

The thundering reply, "Building a snowman," brought the action to a complete halt.

"So," Roxie said, strolling to center front. "What season was it?"

You could almost hear mouths dropping open at the

stupidity of such a question. Roxie waited for an answer.

"Why . . . winter," Claire Neilson mumbled. Claire was the kind of girl who always played up to teachers.

"Winter? Is that right?" Roxie said. "Then I assume it was cold. Had to be, if there was that much snow lying around. All right, then, what was missing in the pantomime?"

"I know! I know!" Hands began waving wildly. And then, remembering the *we're informal*, Susan shouted, "They weren't shivering or anything!"

"Right. Look, people, you've got to show, by facial expression, by movement of your body, the exact conditions. Let's see you shiver. Let's see you rub your mittened hands to warm them. And another thing. I assume if snow is wet enough to pack into snowballs, it has a certain heaviness. You girls looked as though you were tossing around giant marshmallows."

Fran, listening to the criticism, had a feeling of dread. She had finally decided to pantomime a hand-puppet show. But she had practiced very little. The idea of showing emotion hadn't even occurred to her. She'd open the theatre curtains, hold up her fingers as though they had the puppet heads and costumes attached, do a scene, and then close the curtains. It would be terrible, she just knew it.

"Who's next?" Roxie asked.

"Me," Veronica said, and walked to the front.

Fran shifted her eyes from the straight, proud back of her almost-friend to Andrew and Harold. Except for a quick, *get this, now* kind of exchanged look, all eyes were on Veronica.

Please . . . Fran gripped her fingers together . . . please be good! Don't give them any reason to make fun of you!

Veronica, solemn-faced, knelt, and moved her flat hand diagonally up and down several times. She arose, brushed off her knees and legs, peered into the distance, and began walking, carrying a large, heavy object under her right arm. Then she changed her step, lifting her feet and going slowly. She leaned over and knelt on the object she had been carrying.

A sled, Fran thought. But why, then, was Veronica scooping up something, rubbing it onto her arms and shoulders? You wouldn't rub snow over yourself. Now, Veronica seemed to be paddling. *A lifeboat!* But no, Veronica was standing now, balancing. No one would stand up in a lifeboat. Fleetingly, the painting of Washington crossing the Delaware flashed in Fran's mind. But that was silly.

Fran glanced at the rest of the class. Every face had a look of perplexity. Only Roxie looked wise. And approving.

Veronica, as though she were somewhere all alone

in the world, was now shifting her body gracefully, balancing, almost dancing. The way she held her head, you could almost see breezes rippling through her hair. Suddenly she raised her arms protectively, floundered, lowered her head, then raised it for a huge gasp of air. She grabbed the object, which now seemed to be above her, and then, maneuvering, got back down on her knees and paddled.

The pantomime was over. Veronica got up, and looking straight forward, returned to her seat.

"Well!" Roxie said, "If any of you didn't get that, you're just not with the scene!"

I'm not with it, then, Fran thought. It was good, but I don't know what she was doing. She glanced at Veronica beside her. Her look was faraway, as though she couldn't quite bring herself back from wherever she'd been.

"Suggestions?" Roxie prompted. She looked at the class in astonishment as no one volunteered. "You mean," she said, "no one here knows anything about surfing?" She shook her head dolefully. "That must be it, because the action was down pat. She didn't miss a beat." Roxie directed her gaze at Veronica. "How long have you been riding the waves?"

"Never have," Veronica said. "But I've watched them do their wipeouts down at Malibu."

"Then it's even more remarkable." Roxie glanced at the clock. "Oh boy. We'll have to start snapping if we're going to get through all the pantomimes today."

"You," she said, looking at Fran. "Let's have yours."

Fran wished at that moment she had never signed up for drama class. She half opened her mouth to say she wasn't prepared. It was bad enough to get up there at all, but to follow someone good like Veronica!

She went forward, feeling all eyes on her. Oh, how she wished it were over! Trying not to look at the class, she went through the beginning actions. Then she wiggled her fingers furiously as the imaginary puppets, Punch and Judy, began arguing. A movement out in the class attracted her attention. Andrew Willis was waggling his fingers back at her. She forced her mind to the pantomime. Again, when the action got going, she glimpsed Andrew's fingers mimicking her. She shot a glance at Roxie. She was paying attention only to Fran. In a few seconds, Fran closed the curtains with a jerk and went back to her seat, feeling shaky inside.

"Comments?" Roxie asked.

Andrew waved his hand, high this time, and said innocently, "She kept looking out at the audience."

"Yes, a little," Roxie conceded. "Any other comments?"

"Hand puppets," somebody said, and that was all. Fran resolved next time to give more thought and practice to the assignment. And above all, to ignore Andrew.

The two boys waited until last to volunteer, and then they set a speed record with a foolish imitation of William Tell and his son. Andrew was the son and pretended the arrow hit him instead of the apple. He fell, his feet went straight up in the air and dropped with a loud *clomp*. No one laughed except Claire Neilson, who, when she saw she was the only one, pretended she was hiccuping.

"That's all for today," Roxie said, picking up her clipboard. "Now, for next Monday you're to have a dialogue. That's a speech, using two different characters. I don't care what you do, as long as you portray two people and you show a difference in their voices. But remember, you're to do this alone." She looked at Andrew and Harold. "No brother act. I'm going to schedule you clowns first thing, so you'd better be sharp. Okay, scram."

The boys grinned and scooted for the door. Roxie went down the hall toward the reception desk and the girls drifted toward the sunny outdoors.

"Your pantomime was super," Rita said, edging between Fran and Veronica. "Gosh, I could just feel those waves."

"I thought," Sally said, coming along the other side of Veronica, "you didn't know what she was doing." There was a jealous edge to her voice.

"I sort of sensed it," Rita said vaguely.

They pushed through the door. Veronica stopped. "See you Monday," she said abruptly. "Come on, Fran."

Fran felt privileged as the other girls, admiration in their faces, reluctantly left.

"I'll walk you home," Veronica said.

They started down the walk along the side of the pool. Fran decided she'd see if Veronica could stay for lunch at her house. She thought she'd better not mention it until she checked with her mother.

"Hoo hoo, watch me take the wave!" shouted a voice, as Andrew Willis suddenly leaped from behind a clump of bushes. Harold leaped after him.

"Whee!" Andrew waved his arms in wild imitation of Veronica. "Ooopsy . . . I'm going to get my little tootsies wet!"

Harold, not to be outdone, began flailing his arms. "Here comes a nasty big wave . . . whoosh!" And he sprang at the girls.

Veronica didn't budge. "Are you clowns quite finished?" she asked.

Fran could see that the word *clowns* struck home. It was the same word Roxie had used.

"You think you're so sharp!" Andrew sneered. "Who ever heard of surfers around here?"

"Who," Fran said, "ever heard of William Tell hitting his own son?"

"Oh." Andrew was pleased to discover a better target for his sarcasm. "It's little old Frantsy-Pantsy."

"Yeah," Harold echoed, equally glad to find weaker prey. "Frantsy-Pantsy."

I'm not going to show I care, Fran thought. But was she a good enough actress to disguise her feelings?

Veronica, without taking her eyes from the boys, said, "Frances, what are the full names of these people?"

Fran, surprised, managed to stammer, "Andrew Willis and Harold Holbrook."

"Oh, yes." Veronica cleared her throat. "Now I remember. Silly Willy and Harold Halfwit." She gave them a look of disdain. "Why don't you two creeps buzz off while your cages are being cleaned?"

The boys stared, speechless.

"Get lost," Veronica advised, quickly following up her advantage.

Andrew, still at a loss for words, decided to take action. He made a dash for his tormentor. Veronica waited until the very last second and stepped aside. Andrew went hurtling down the sidewalk, barely

keeping his balance. Harold, a little slower to take action, whipped past Fran, giving her shoulder a slap and spinning her almost to the ground.

"We'll fix you smart alecks!" Andrew called, fury in his voice.

"We're really worried," Veronica replied. "Hah," she said, walking in the opposite direction, toward the street, "amateurs."

Rubbing her shoulder, Fran didn't feel quite so brave. "They're really mad now," she said. "It's hard telling what they'll do."

"The thing is, don't give them a chance to do anything. Or," Veronica said, "if they catch you unaware, roll with the punches. I'll show you how. Ever hear of Crash Calahan?"

Fran shook her head.

"He's a stunt man. Lived down the street from us in Hollywood. Used to do the dangerous parts in films. You know, so the star wouldn't get hurt. Crash showed us neighborhood kids some of his tricks. They're simple, once you get the hang of them. Of course, it takes practice."

"Why did they call him Crash?"

Veronica gave a little jump and pulled a leaf from a tree. "Even the best of stunt men miss sometimes," she said. She blew on the leaf against her lips and made it whistle. "Hey," she said, "speaking of crashes, watch out!"

Fran's first thought was that the boys were back again. But in the instant before she ducked behind a tree, the image registered. It was only Chip, speeding down the sidewalk on his bike. He squealed to a stop.

"Can't you be more careful?" Fran asked irritably, stepping from behind the tree. "You could have hit us." Chip seemed not to hear. He was staring, transfixed, at Veronica.

"This is Chip, Veronica," Fran said reluctantly. "My brother."

"Hi, kid," Veronica said pleasantly.

Chip licked his lips and took a deep breath. "Are you really from Hollywood, where the stars come from?"

"You'd better believe it."

"I do!" Chip breathed. Fran had never heard such awe in his voice.

Veronica smiled and shifted a little. "It's just an expression, kiddo."

"Chip," Fran said, wishing he'd leave, "I thought you were going to try to earn some money today, for that Alamo game. How come you're riding around?"

"No one wants to hire me," Chip said. "You coming to our house for lunch, Veronica?"

Now Fran was really irritated. She turned her back on Chip. "I was just going to ask you, Veronica," she said. "Can you?"

"Gee, sorry, but I'm supposed to meet my mother on her lunch hour and buy a new swimsuit. Some other time, maybe."

"See you!" Chip said, turning his bike and pedaling away. "Come over soon, Veronica!"

"He's a cute boy," Veronica said with a smile.

Fran couldn't have agreed less. "No boy," she said, "is cute."

6

Andrew Does His Dialogue

REMEMBERING HER PROMISE, Roxie eyed the boys that next Monday morning. "One of you, I don't care which, will start us off on dialogues today," she said. "Who wants to begin?"

"I will," Andrew Willis said.

Fran, sitting with Veronica across the aisle from the boys, sensed that they were up to no good. Andrew's face had that look of exaggerated innocence she knew so well, and Harold looked as though he were about to explode from bottled-up laughter.

Andrew swaggered to the front of the room, and with one brief glance at his buddy, who still seemed about to burst, recited rapidly:

"Mary, Mary, you must get up."
"Oh, Mother, I'm not able."
"Mary, Mary, you must get up,
We need the sheet for the table."

In the hush that followed, Andrew bolted for his chair, where he sat rigidly, arms folded, staring straight ahead. Harold, seated beside him, laughed crazily, his face buried in his folded arms.

Roxie strolled to the front of the room, showing no emotion. She looked at Andrew. "That's it?" she asked.

Andrew widened his eyes in pretended innocence. "You said you didn't care what it was, as long as it had two people talking." He glanced quickly at Harold, who by now was bent over double. "Mine did."

Roxie gave a lift to her eyebrows. "True. But where were your characterizations? One voice sounded the same as the other." She walked around the room, as though considering. "What was the girl's line again?"

Clearly Andrew had not expected this kind of reaction. To be yelled at, yes. To be sent from the room, possibly. But to be taken seriously, never. He unfolded his arms and shifted in his seat.

Roxie stood with hands on her hips like a football coach, waiting. "I asked, what was the girl's line?"

Andrew moistened his lips and sneaked glances at the girls around him. This time, instead of giggling at his antics, they were eyeing him, waiting to see how he would get out of this situation. Andrew shifted again, and stared down at his sneakers.

"Since you can't seem to recall that one line," Roxie said, "we'd better have the whole poem again. Come on, Willis, up to the front of the room."

Andrew gave a desperate glance at the door. Finally, he arose and shuffled to the front of the room, where, with eyes downcast and voice barely above a mumble, he started the recitation.

After the second line, Roxie clapped him on the shoulder. "That's it — the girl's response, 'Oh, Mother, I'm not able.' Now, to make the poem intelligible, you've got to change your voice on that line so we realize it's a different person speaking."

Again, Andrew's eyes flickered toward the door. Next he glanced at the clock, as though by some magic, the hour would be over. Then, gazing downward, he muttered, "I can't do it."

"The line," Roxie said, standing firm, "is 'Oh Mother, I'm not able.' Say it, now, in a high-pitched voice."

Andrew raised his head defiantly. "Oh, Mother," he growled, "I'm not able."

The class screamed with laughter.

Roxie smiled grimly. "I said girl . . . not *gorilla*." Again, the class laughed.

"Come now," Roxie said, "you can do it. Haven't you ever imitated a girl?"

For a split second, Andrew's eyes met Fran's, and she knew he was remembering the same thing she was. On the last day of school he had imitated a girl's voice with no trouble at all. His voice had been high-pitched when he said, "I'm Veronica Tongue-Twist. And I'm all dressed up to meet my new classmates."

"If you can't do it today," Roxie was saying, "I'll only make a note to have you do it next time. So you might as well get it over with."

Andrew took a deep breath. Staring at the back wall, he blurted, "Mary, Mary, you must get up."

And changing his voice, "Oh, Mother, I'm not able."

He finished the poem and bolted for his chair, where he scrunched down until his chin rested on his chest.

"I knew all along you could do it," Roxie said with a satisfied little smile as she made a check mark on her clipboard paper. "Who's next? Oh, yes, Holbrook. We don't want to forget you."

Harold, who had become considerably subdued during the last part of Andrew's ordeal, now had the look of a drowning dog.

"I can't . . . today," he stammered. "I have a . . . a sunburn."

Roxie looked him over. "Where?" she asked. "On your vocal chords?"

"I feel bad."

"That's understandable." She scribbled at her clipboard. "We'll look forward to hearing from you first thing Thursday."

Harold nodded dumbly.

"Let's continue," Roxie said. "For a change of pace, could we have something a little more challenging? Who'll volunteer?"

There was a general shifting and squirming as each girl hoped another would step up front.

Claire Neilson raised her hand. "I have a dialogue," she said with an air of importance. "I took it from Shakespeare. Is that all right?"

"It's all right with me if it's all right with Shakespeare," Roxie replied. And then in a softer tone, "Do you understand the selection?"

"Oh, yes," Claire said in her prim little voice.

Veronica leaned closer to Fran. "Bet you anything it's from *Romeo and Juliet*," she whispered. "That's just her speed."

Claire Neilson went to the front and stood straight as a ballerina, toes angled, and fingers laced at her waist.

"This is a selection from *Romeo and Juliet*," she said.

"I knew it," Veronica muttered. "Brace yourself."

"The scene," Claire said, "takes place on the balcony. Romeo speaks first:

"Lady, by yonder blessed moon I swear,
That tips with silver all these fruit-tree tops,—"

Claire spoke the lines in a gutteral tone. Now she smiled in a sticky-sweet way and touched her clasped hands to her chin as she said:

"O! swear not by the moon, the inconstant moon,
That monthly changes in her circled orb,
Lest that thy love prove likewise variable."

"What," Claire answered, shifting position, and in the lower voice, *"shall I swear by?"*

Again, her hands went up as she replied,

"Do not swear at all;
Or, if thou wilt, swear by thy gracious self,

And . . . and" . . . she looked at the ceiling as though the forgotten words were printed there . . . *"And I'll believe thee."*

Roxie closed her eyes briefly. After a deep breath, she said, "Are there any more selections from Shakespeare?"

"I have one," Veronica said, rising. "It's from *Macbeth.*"

Fran stared, open-mouthed. Before class, Veronica

had said she was going to do something from *Treasure Island*. "Check this," Veronica murmured, as she edged in front of Fran and went to the front of the room.

"The setting," she announced, "is a cavern. The witches are stirring their brew in the cauldron, and at the end, Macbeth enters." She turned to Roxie. "I'll cut some of the speeches."

Roxie nodded.

Veronica screwed her face into a horrible grimace and bent stiffly over an imaginary cauldron, stirring with clawlike hands.

"Double, double toil and trouble," she intoned in a screechy voice, *"Fire burn and cauldron bubble."*

She shifted to impersonate another witch, and in an even more hideous voice continued,

> *"Fillet of a fenny snake,*
> *In the cauldron boil and bake;*
> *Eye of newt and toe of frog,*
> *Wool of bat and tongue of dog."*

Then, with hunched shoulders, Veronica lifted her head and peered wickedly around.

> *"By the pricking of my thumbs,*
> *Something wicked this way comes.*
> *Open, locks,*
> *Whoever knocks!"*

After the screech of the final words Veronica, now as Macbeth, raised herself proudly, and in a deep, dignified voice said:

"*How now, you secret, black, and midnight hags!*
What is it you do? An eternal curse fall on you!"

Then, again, as a witch, she cackled:

"*Show his eyes, and grieve his heart;*
Come like shadows, so depart!"

On the final line, Veronica crept down the aisle, clawlike hands extended. Sally and Rita cowered as though they might be attacked, and even Andrew and Harold shrank back as she passed.

Veronica dropped into her seat, breathing a bit rapidly.

Roxie passed her hand over her face and gave her head a shake. "I'll say one thing for this class," she said. "It's full of surprises." She sank into a chair at the end of the first row. "Do you think, just for variety, we could have an everyday sort of dialogue now? Nancy, how about you?"

"My scene is from *Little Women*," Nancy said, with a worried little frown.

"I couldn't ask for more. Shoot," Roxie said.

As Nancy made her way forward, Fran whispered to Veronica, "How come you changed to that witch scene?"

"I just felt," Veronica murmured, "that Shakespeare deserved a second chance."

Fran held back as one girl after the other volunteered. It was frightening to go up before the class. It was even worse to keep waiting, knowing that eventually she'd have to do it.

Finally she got up the courage. "My dialogue is from *Heidi*," she said. In spite of herself, she darted a glance at the boys. They looked as though the only thing they wanted was for class to be over.

Fran had practiced using different voices for Heidi and Clara, and also different gestures. She had been quite impressed with herself at home. But now, she was trembling so much, it seemed her voices got all mixed up.

Still, the class appeared interested. As Fran finished she wished she could begin all over, and do it better.

Because time was running short, there were few comments.

"Before you tear out of here," Roxie said, "I want to make an announcement. On Thursday, there will be no outside assignment because we're going to talk about makeup, props, and so on. Then a week from today we'll have tryouts for the play. After that, we'll be rehearsing."

"What's the play? What's the play?" voices shouted.

"You'll find out Monday," Roxie said with a smile.

"I'm not sure," Fran said to Veronica as they strolled outside afterward, "that I'll even want to be in the play. I get so scared."

Veronica shrugged. "Everyone's scared at first. But you soon get over it."

"Well, maybe." Fran wasn't convinced. "Do you think we'll all get parts in the play?"

Veronica hooted. "Are you kidding? Of course everyone will get a part." She stopped to scratch her bare knee. "Even if it's just a servant or something. The parents would squawk otherwise." She straightened and looked at Fran. "I don't suppose you're wearing a swimsuit under that dress."

Fran stared. "A swimsuit? No. Why?"

"Well," Veronica said, "I'm wearing mine. This is the best time to go in, before the pool is crowded."

Fran felt annoyed. "Why didn't you ask me beforehand?" she asked. "I could have."

They had reached the gate entrance to the pool. Veronica stepped out of her right loafer and stooped to shake a quarter and a dime into her hand. "I wanted to call," she said, wiggling her foot back into the shoe, "but there are about a zillion Sanderses in the phone book. You'll have to give me your number."

"It's . . . we're the ones on Oak Street. Wait!"

Veronica, who had already started toward the bathhouse, turned and paused.

"Why don't you come and have lunch with me and then we can come back and swim this afternoon?"

"Can't today," Veronica said with a cheery wave. "I'll call you."

"But . . ." She was gone.

Fran hooked her fingers through the links of the fence and absently watched the divers. A girl about Fran's age was practicing her jackknife. By the time Debbie came back from camp, she'd probably be an expert diver. She was going to take archery, too, and learn to sail. Fran tightened her grip until her fingers smarted. Debbie would be changed. She knew it. She'd have friends who had been at camp, girls who could share all the remember-whens.

And who would Fran have? No one. Veronica was like a fish in still water who glided to your side. But when you reached out, she was away in a flash.

I don't care, Fran thought, turning to go. She rubbed her fingers. I can get along without anyone. I'll try to get a good part in the play. And then . . . She didn't know what she'd do then. She didn't even know what she'd do the rest of the afternoon.

7

The Lightning Bug Maneuver

THE PROBLEM of what to do was solved by Mrs. Sanders after lunch.

"How about finishing the dress you started making during spring vacation?" she asked Fran. "It only needs to be marked and hemmed, remember."

"I'll help," Chip said eagerly. "I'll thread the needle and hand you pins and things. If you'll pay me."

"Why can't you do it just to be nice?" Fran wanted to know.

"Because I need the money. I still have thirty-five cents to go before I can get an Alamo game."

"Chip," his mother said, "you can't expect to get

money for doing these simple little things. You have to exert yourself."

"Could I sell lemonade? That would be exerting myself."

Mrs. Sanders laughed. "Are you sure you have the strength?"

"I guess so," Chip said good-naturedly. "If Fran will help me set it up."

Before Fran could reply, Mrs. Sanders said, "Now, Chip, you just trot out and find that old card table in the garage. Wash it off, get a chair, and fix things for yourself."

"And make a sign," Fran suggested. "There's cardboard in my desk."

Chip came back with the cardboard and a crayon. "Instead of saying *lemonade,* could I say *booze?*" he called to his mother in the kitchen.

"No, you may not," was the reply. "Chip, I don't know where you pick up these things. You'd better say *cold drink* anyway. I see there's just cherry-flavored mix here."

"That's good," Chip said. "I don't care much for lemonade, to tell you the truth." He darted outside with the sign and came back to pick up the rest of the supplies. "Here's the mail," he said. "There's a letter for you, Fran."

"Debbie!" she shouted, recognizing the hand-writing.

The letter, on camp stationery with a bow-and-arrow border, read:

Dear Goon Girl [their nickname for each other]: Camp is okay, but I get pretty tired. We have to get up at six and take a dip BEFORE BREAKFAST! And then we eat and after that have archery or stuff like that. Then we have lunch and crafts or letter writing and at night we go on scavenger hunts or sing around a campfire, etc. etc. etc. etc. and then believe it or not we go to bed almost before dark. How is everyone? I am tanned. You won't know me. My hair has grown, it seems like two inches. I started to get a wart but it went away. What kind of costumes have you worn so far at drama class? Write soon.

Your friend,
Debbie the Goon Girl

Fran felt a wave of loneliness for her friend. She wished Debbie would walk into the room right now. There was so much they could talk about! They used to spend hours comparing notes or making plans. With Debbie gone there was a big emptiness.

It was all very well to say you should have more

than just one friend, but friends were hard to get. A best friend had to be someone who was always there. (Debbie couldn't help being sent to camp.) And a best friend was someone who told you everything.

Veronica's face popped into Fran's mind. Fran liked her. She liked her a lot. But Veronica didn't try to be a best or even a good friend. She disappeared. She didn't talk much about herself, just about things that happened. There was something both strange and familiar about her. Who was she? Veronica didn't even seem to know, herself.

While her mother marked the hem, Fran dutifully turned, not lifting her arms. Actresses, she had read somewhere, often had to stand for hours, being fitted. *"What kind of costumes have you worn so far?"* Debbie had asked. Fran frowned. If Debbie only knew what they were doing in class, she'd be disgusted. It wasn't glamorous at all. But the play . . .

"Turn please," her mother said.

Fran shifted. The play, at least, would be exciting. Maybe she'd be a princess? No, that wasn't likely. There were too many really pretty girls in the class. Maybe — what a thought — maybe she wouldn't be in it at all, in spite of what Veronica had said! Maybe there wouldn't be enough parts for everyone. On the other hand, what if she got a part in the play and forgot her lines in front of the whole audience? And Debbie! Debbie would be back by then! Fran got a funny, fluttery feeling right in her middle.

"That's it," her mother said, rising to her feet. "Can you manage now?"

"I guess so," Fran said. "I'm glad it's not a full skirt." She finished hemming in less than an hour.

"Very pretty," Mr. Sanders commented when Fran brought it out to the patio after dinner. "I can see it's been a busy day here in the old corral."

"It sure was," Chip said. "My cold drink stand did a lot of business."

"Oh?" Fran asked. "How much money did you make?"

Chip crossed his legs on the outdoor rocker and started it in motion. "You don't understand. You have to give away free samples to get started in business. And by the time all the guys in the neighborhood — "

Mrs. Sanders opened the screen door. "There's a phone call. It's Veronica."

"Really?" Fran flung her dress over her arm and jumped up.

"She wants to talk with Chip," Mrs. Sanders said.

"Chip!" Fran couldn't believe her ears.

"Me?" Chip's eyes widened in astonishment. He leaped from the rocker and it teetered back and forth crazily. "I wonder why me?" he said as he raced into the house.

Fran stared at her mother. Mrs. Sanders lifted her eyebrows and shrugged.

In a moment Chip bounded out, quivering with excitement. "Boy oh boy, this is my lucky day!" he announced. "Veronica found a newspaper clipping about some laboratory that wants to buy lightning bugs and she said she'd drop it off in a few minutes, on her way some place. She knows how I'm trying to earn money."

"Lightning bugs?" Mrs. Sanders said.

"Lightning bugs?" Mr. Sanders echoed. "Why would a laboratory want lightning bugs?"

"It must be some joke," Fran said.

"No, it's for real." Chip, beside himself with excitement, darted around the house. "I'll wait for her out front," he called.

In just a few minutes, he came back, pulling Veronica by the hand. "Tell them," he urged. "It's not a joke, is it?"

Fran, remembering her manners, introduced Veronica to her parents. Veronica, so sure of herself around kids, now hung back shyly.

"What's all this about a laboratory wanting lightning bugs?" Mr. Sanders asked with a smile.

Veronica twitched her shoulders in embarrassment. "It says fireflies," she mumbled, "but I guess it's the same as lightning bugs. It's for, uh . . ." Again she twitched. "They want them for . . . uh . . ."

"Space research!" Chip exclaimed, peering at the clipping. "It says, 'The tail light of the glowworm may prove useful in detecting mic . . . mic . . .'"

"'Microorganisms in outer space,'" Mr. Sanders read, over Chip's shoulder.

"And get this!" Chip's voice rose to a squeal. "They're paying a half-cent each! Boy, and our yard is lousy with them, or will be, once it gets dark."

Mr. Sanders was still absorbed in the article. "It says they need a half-million of them. It's some laboratory in Lyons. I never heard of such a thing!"

"A half-million!" Chip breathed.

Mr. Sanders gave a wry smile. "Imagine . . . a bounty on fireflies. That's the space age for you!"

"Well, 'bye. I've got to leave now," Veronica said.

"No!" Chip grabbed her hand. "Stay! I'll find a jar for you."

"Yes, stay!" Fran urged. Maybe if Veronica got used to her parents now she wouldn't feel strange about coming back again.

Veronica wavered. "Well, my mother is out in the car," she said. "We just stopped by on the way to the market."

"Could you ask her to pick you up on the way back?" Fran suggested.

"Okay." Veronica looked pleased.

Fran, Chip, and Veronica rushed around the house to the driveway. "Mother," Veronica said to the pretty blonde woman smiling from behind the wheel, "this is Fran, and Chip. They want to know if I can stay here while you shop."

"We need her help," Chip said, "to catch half a million lightning bugs."

Mrs. Lindquist laughed, looking even prettier. "All right. I'll pick you up in an hour, Veronica." She turned on the ignition. "Nice to have met you, Fran and Chip."

The girls and Chip waved her off and ran into the house to find jars.

"It's lucky my mom saves stuff like this," Chip said, rummaging through a cabinet with fruitcake tins, coffee cans, and other odds and ends. "This mayonnaise jar should hold a hundred at least."

"Won't the bugs die with the lid on?" Veronica asked.

"Naw. You punch holes in the lid. And add a little grass. Hey," Chip asked, "didn't you ever catch lightning bugs before?"

"We don't have them on the coast."

"Just watch me," Chip said. "I'll show you how to catch them bare-handed."

He acted, Fran thought, like a big-game hunter about to trap an elephant.

8

Veronica's Secret

BEFORE HE WENT TO BED, Chip insisted on counting the lightning bugs. "There are exactly one hundred and twenty," he told his mother. "I'd like to keep the jars in my room tonight. These lights would be handy in case we have a storm and a power failure."

"You think of everything," Mrs. Sanders said. "Now, off to bed. Fran?"

"It's not quite *my* bedtime," she reminded. "Besides, I'd like to write a letter to Debbie before we drive to Lyons tomorrow."

"Goodness, it's only three miles," her mother said. "But go ahead." She went off with Chip.

Fran wrote the date at the top of her flower-printed stationery. She found it hard to concentrate on thoughts of Debbie. Her mind kept returning to Ve-

95

ronica and her surprisingly pretty mother. It was funny, but Fran had the feeling that Veronica had been glad her mother had gone off instead of staying to be introduced to Fran's parents. Oh well, it didn't mean anything. She sighed and began:

Dear Goon Girl:

Camp sounds like a lot of fun. Be sure to remember everything that happens so you can tell me when you get back. Maybe you can sleep overnight.

She idly clicked the top of her ball-point pen. What could she say next? Something about class. But she didn't want to get into a long description of the pantomimes and dialogues. Debbie wouldn't be all that interested anyway. Andrew and Harold! Debbie would be amazed to hear they were in drama class too. Just then she thought of something odd. The boys hadn't bothered them today after class, in spite of their threats last week. Probably it was because Andrew had been so embarrassed about his dialogue and all. He never reformed. She wrote:

Guess who's taking drama too? Andrew and Harold. (The creeps.) And they're even worse than they were at school last year if you can imagine such a thing. Well, I've got to go to bed now.

Your friend,
Fran, the Goon Girl

P.S. Remember Veronica? That new girl? She's taking drama too. She's not so bad.

Fran paused. She wanted to add, *I think you'll like her.* But it simply wasn't true. There was almost nothing about Veronica that Debbie would approve of. She didn't like girls who were the least bit different or who didn't care about their looks. And while Fran found it kind of exciting that there was something mysterious about Veronica, Debbie would hate it. The only secrets she could stand were her own.

Fran folded the letter. She was going to keep on being friendly to Veronica. She liked her. But when Debbie came back? She shrugged. She'd worry about that when it happened.

The phone rang just as Mrs. Sanders came back into the room. "Margaret!" she said after the first hello. "I've been wanting to come over and give you some escape. How's Clara?"

Fran addressed the envelope. "I'm sure they'd love it," Mrs. Sanders was saying, "and the change would be nice for all of us." Fran wished they'd finish talking so she could find out what it was they would love.

It was better than she had expected. Aunt Margaret had offered to take her and Chip to the beach and make the lightning-bug stop on the way.

"Could Veronica go too?" Fran asked.

"I should think so. Why don't you call Veronica now and see? Your Aunt Margaret won't mind."

Veronica said at once she could go.

The next day at the beach, Chip gallantly offered to divide his earnings four ways. He was sitting cross-legged in the sand next to the blanket. "Sixty cents," he counted. "Fifteen cents for each of the lightning-bug catchers, and fifteen cents for the lady who made this trip possible. Does anyone have any change?"

"Tell you what," Aunt Margaret said. "You three divide the money, because you did me a favor by coming along. Without you this trip wouldn't have been possible because I hate going to the beach alone."

"Count me out too," Veronica said. "I don't want to be paid. It was fun catching those critters."

"You can keep my share too," Fran added, not to be outdone. "Use it to help buy your Alamo game."

"How," Chip said grandly, with a wide sweep of his arms, "can I ever thank you?"

Aunt Margaret laughed. "Easy. You can help me gather pebbles for a collage I have in mind."

"Aunt Margaret is an art teacher," Fran explained to Veronica. "She's always making interesting things."

"I'll start collecting right now," Chip said, putting the dimes into his shoe.

"Relax," Aunt Margaret advised, settling down on the blanket. "The sun's so nice just now." But Chip was already bounding down to the water's edge.

"He's so energetic," Fran said, stretching out beside her aunt. "Mother says she could run her washer for a week on the energy Chip puts out in an hour." She propped herself on her elbows and looked at Veronica. "Aren't you going to sun yourself?"

"I guess so." Veronica took off her shirt and jeans. Her swimsuit was striped.

"How's the play coming along?" Aunt Margaret asked, flicking a few grains of sand from the blanket. "Have you been cast yet?"

"Oh, no. Tryouts are Monday." Fran shifted to make room for Veronica. "How do you try out, anyway?" she asked her friend.

"Oh, usually the director tells about the play and characters. Then she has a bunch of people read and then another bunch and then she tells who gets what part. That's all."

"What if you don't like the part she gives you?" Fran asked.

"You just take it and like it." Veronica blew her bangs away from her eyes. "That's show biz."

"Anyway, I'll be glad when we *do* something," Fran said. "I'm tired of just loosening up."

Aunt Margaret, eyes closed, smiled. "That sounds like the tin man in *The Wizard of Oz*, only of course you people aren't rusty."

"Rusty!" Veronica hooted. "We haven't done anything to get rusty about. No technique, no nothing."

"What's technique?" Fran asked timidly.

Veronica flopped on her back. "Technique," she said in her old bored voice, "is something you should know before you get on stage. I guess Roxie figures she'll just teach it as she goes along."

"Yes, but what is it?" Fran persisted.

"How to enter a room, for one thing," Veronica said.

Fran laughed. "Enter a room! Why, you just walk in."

"Oh?" Veronica, still on her back, crossed her legs and waggled one foot in the air. "How would you walk in if you were an old, sick person? The same way you'd walk in if you were a young girl in love?"

Fran chewed her lip thoughtfully. "I guess not."

Veronica continued, "Would you enter the same way if you were a prowler looking for jewels as you would if you owned the house and had just come in for a book?"

"I never thought of that." Fran felt as though panels were being moved to reveal a new, secret world.

"There's even a technique to opening a door," Veronica went on. With a catlike movement she sprang to her feet and faced them. "When you're entering from a side door, you turn the knob with your upstage hand." She demonstrated. "But after you're in the room, you reach back and close it with your downstage hand. Know why?"

"Why?"

"So your body is facing the audience at all times."

"My word!" Aunt Margaret, leaning on her elbow, was wide-eyed behind her dark glasses. "And it all looks so simple when you watch a play."

"That's the idea," Veronica said, flopping down.

"Veronica, have you studied acting a great deal?" Aunt Margaret asked. "But you must have."

"Oh . . ." Veronica made lines in the sand with her finger. "I've had a few lessons. When my mother refused to go back, Alice started concentrating on me."

"Alice," Fran explained to her aunt, "is Veronica's grandmother."

Aunt Margaret looked puzzled. "Go back, Veronica? Where, dear?"

Veronica squirmed. "She was in the movies when she was a kid. Alice thought she'd go back when she was eighteen, but she got married instead." She smoothed over the lines in the sand. "Then Alice tried to get me into TV. As a surprise for my folks, she said.

But when they found out about it, Dad asked for a job transfer. So that's why we're here."

Aunt Margaret's face was all concern. "Did you want to stay, Veronica, and become an actress?"

"Not that way. Who wants to be introduced around as 'Carol Lane's little girl. A real talent!'? I might want to act someday. But I'm not sure. Hey, Chip!" she said as he came to join them. "Did you find any good pebbles?"

"Sure," Chip said. "But I need someone to help carry them."

"I will." With one of her quick leaps, Veronica was on her feet and whirling down the beach, with Chip pattering behind her like a puppy.

"Gee," Fran exclaimed, leaning on her knees and watching them, "I never dreamed Veronica was so exciting. Imagine having a mother who's a movie star!"

"Well, not quite. Rather, a child actress. And she evidently wasn't very happy, being one."

"I don't see why not. Just think of all the fun — "

"It's hard work, Fran. And she probably didn't get to do the things that an average girl does."

"But what she did was so much better!"

Aunt Margaret shrugged. "She must not have thought so. At any rate, she didn't want the same sort of life for her daughter."

Fran thought about that. "Someday, though, I'll

bet Veronica will be a movie star. Boy, wait until I tell
Debbie and all the kids!"

"Tell them what, Fran?"

Fran stared at her aunt. "Why, about Veronica's
mother and all."

Aunt Margaret took off her dark glasses. "Are you
going to tell them?"

"Of course! I mean . . ." Fran looked away from
her aunt. "Don't you think I should?"

Her aunt didn't answer. Fran knew what she was
thinking. Fran was thinking the same thing. If Veronica had wanted it spread around that her mother had
been famous, and that she knew show people, she'd
have said so. She had told them here, only because
they had asked, and because she trusted them.

"Don't you think, perhaps, you should let Veronica
make friends her own way, and on her own merits?"
Aunt Margaret asked, after a moment. "Wouldn't that
be best?"

"I guess so," Fran agreed. "But you know, Veronica
seems kind of odd, until you know her, and Debbie
might not give her a chance. But if I told her about
Veronica's mother, she'd be more likely . . ." Her voice
trailed off.

"Fran." And now Aunt Margaret's voice was softer.

"Are you afraid of Debbie? Afraid of losing her friendship, I mean?"

Fran looked down at the shadow between her arms. "I guess so, in a way."

"You know, even friendship has limits. You can't let someone else take over your life." Aunt Margaret sat up and watched the two figures coming back along the beach. "My word, they're loaded down. Maybe we can all make a collage. Or a rock garden."

9

Lovely Lovely Lipstick

"ALL SET?" Roxie asked Thursday morning. "We're going to get down to business today." She passed out mimeographed papers.

"Here's a list of stage definitions you should know," she said. "We'll talk about some of them briefly and go into them more as we rehearse. We could spend the whole summer learning about backstage work, but we just haven't time. Not when we're putting on a play in a few weeks. You'll have to learn as you go along."

Fran shot a glance at Veronica. It was practically the same thing she had said at the beach.

Rita Jones waggled her hand in the air. "I thought we were going to have make-up today," she said.

"We will, as soon as we romp over these paragraphs," Roxie said. "Doreen, would you begin reading?"

"Props. There are two kinds of props — hand props and set props," Doreen read in a loud, clear voice. "Hand props are items actors carry, such as fans, handkerchiefs, pipes." Someone giggled. "Set props," she continued, "are items which are placed on the stage, and which may be used by the actors, such as dishes, books, et cetera." She sat down.

"Is that clear?" Roxie asked. "When we do our play, our prop committee will be responsible for the set props. But each actor or actress gets and keeps track of his own hand props. Questions? No? Then continue, Laura."

"Furniture and Set Decoration," Laura read. "Usually, each piece of furniture, whether it's a sofa, chair, or table, has a special reason for being on stage and is put to use. Set decoration, however, such as pillows, pictures, vases of flowers, help set the mood of the play and show what type of person lives in that room." Laura glanced around and sat down.

"Okay?" Roxie asked.

"I don't get it," Sally Forsythe said. "How could a vase of flowers tell you who lived there?" She was rewarded with a burst of subdued giggles from the girls around her.

Roxie was unperturbed. "Who can answer that?" she asked.

Fran glanced at Veronica, but a voice on the other side of her said, "I think it would tell a lot." It was Nancy Remberg, a quiet, dark-haired girl.

"All right, explain it," Roxie said.

Nancy stood up. "If there were small delicate vases of . . . oh, violets . . . well, you'd expect to see a delicate woman." Fran liked the quiet dignity of Nancy, who didn't seem to mind Rita's and Sally's haughty stares.

"Can you go on?" Roxie asked. "You're on the right track."

Nancy thought a moment. "A tall vase of bright red roses might mean that an actress lived in the room."

Roxie nodded. "What if it were a man's study?"

"I don't think there'd be any flowers at all. Just maybe books and pictures . . . and maybe a world globe."

"Very good. Who wants to read the next paragraph? Yes, Claire."

"Costumes." Claire read in a phony nicey-nice voice. "Costumes should be chosen to portray the character's age, personality, and position in life. Dark colors usually indicate dignity, bright colors a strong personality, and pastels, youth and innocence."

"That's me," Harold said, just loud enough to be heard.

"Care should be taken," Claire continued, "to choose colors which blend with other costume colors and which contrast with the color of the set." She gave Harold a withering look before sitting down.

"Any questions or comments?" Roxie asked. "Then take these pages home and read everything. Now, on to make-up." She flipped open the hinges of a long aluminum toolbox. "Come up here, everyone." The class crowded around. Roxie moved to the end of the long table and turned the box so that it faced her students.

"Here are the essentials of stage make-up," she said. "Harold, why do actors wear make-up?"

"I guess they wear it to look better," he said. "So I won't need any."

"Right," Andrew said. "Nothing could help your looks."

"Cut the clowning," Roxie commanded. "Or I'll make you both up to look like girls. What's another use for stage make-up, anybody?"

"To make them look like someone different . . . or older?" Cindy asked. "Like if a girl wants to look like an old hag . . ."

"Okay. To help build character." Roxie placed several tubes of make-up on the table. "These are foundation colors. Obviously, you put one of them on first. Then, you may add rouge, eye liner, shadow, lipstick." She placed those items on the table. "Last, you lay on face powder with a puff. Don't rub, just press it on. Then you brush off the excess with one of these. That's right, baby brushes. Now, when it comes to removing make-up, you slather on lots of cold cream, and then tissue it off."

She looked around. "Ready to go to it?"

"Yes!" shouted the girls.

In the mad scramble to find chairs at the long tables, Fran and Veronica got separated.

"Keep the easel mirrors in the center of the table so people on both sides can use them," Roxie said. "Nancy, please pass out these directions."

The directions were sketches with dotted lines and arrows where the make-up should be applied.

Roxie put a tube of foundation on the table between every two or three people. "You'll have to share these supplies today. We won't worry about correct shades. Okay, everybody get a glob of make-up in the palm of the hand. The left hand, unless you're left-handed."

"I'm left-handed," Claire announced. "What shall I do?"

"Make like a tree and leave," Andrew suggested.

Doreen, next to Claire, murmured that she should use her right hand. Claire, with a sniff, did so.

"Now," Roxie said, "with your right fingertips — your left, Claire — put a dab of foundation on your cheeks, your chin, your forehead, and if there's any left, on your neck." She paused. "Go on, boys, it won't burn. Now, with the fingertips of both hands, smooth the foundation under your eyes . . . gently . . . up, over your cheekbones, and now, all over your face. You girls with bangs ought to wear a ribbon or scarf or something to hold back the hair."

Fran leaned forward and looked across at Veronica at the next table. She had brought a headband. Without all that hair in her face, and with her glasses off, she looked like a different girl. Rita, sitting opposite Fran, kept pushing her dark bangs aside. They had grease paint all along the edges.

Roxie strolled around plopping down jars of rouge. "Take just a tiny bit," she said, "and put three dots on the cheeks, forming a triangle. Then blend it in. Now, boys, go ahead. You have to wear make-up if you want to be an actor."

"I never did want to be," Harold said. "Andrew made me sign up for this class."

"Well, that's what you get for being half of a comedy team," Roxie said.

She passed out eye shadow. "I'm sure you girls know all about this, from TV commercials. Smooth it over your upper lid, angled toward the eyebrow. Then, with these pencils, draw a line next to your lower and upper lashes, and for heaven's sake, don't stab yourselves in the eye. If you need help, raise your hand."

For the next few minutes, there was a lot of peering into the mirrors and squeals of dismay or delight.

Fran's hand trembled as she carefully moved the pencil along the right lashes, and then held down the left lid, which wouldn't stay shut, and did that eye. She was thrilled with the effect. She looked at least ten years older.

"Here are lipstick samples, which you may keep," Roxie said, "in the interest of hygiene. But you'd better sock them away for a while. I don't want to hear any complaints from your mothers."

Rita and Sally bent their heads together, comparing shades, and finally trading.

"That's as far as we're going today, as a class," Roxie

said. "Now I'd like to demonstrate a basic way to age a person. Do we have a volunteer?"

Fran stared at her reflection. She didn't want to spoil that wonderful new look.

"Anyone?" Roxie urged. "Veronica, good."

Fran felt Veronica walk past her, but she didn't see her face until she got beside Roxie. Then, it was all Fran could do to keep from gasping. With her hair back, and make-up on, Veronica was positively pretty!

"Good job of make-up," Roxie said with admiration. "Wonderful touches. You'd make a perfect ingenue. An ingenue," she explained to the class, "is the young woman in a play. Now, we should really take all this off, but to save time we'll just remove the rouge and eye shadow. On her cheeks, we'll smooth on gray shadow. Up close, it just looks like smudges, but with stage lights, and from a distance, her cheeks would look hollow. Now, compress your lips, Veronica." Roxie drew an eyebrow pencil along the lines formed on Veronica's face. "Wrinkle your forehead." Again, she followed the lines.

Roxie spun Veronica's hair into a knot on top of her head and held it there for the class to see. "This would be sprayed gray, to age her more," Roxie said. "There are other touches, but it depends on just what type of old person you're playing. Okay, thanks, Veronica."

Veronica went back to her seat and started smearing cleansing cream on her face.

"Everyone clean up now," Roxie said. "And don't spare the cream. Girls, I'm going to have a door check, so don't try to sneak out of here with eye make-up on."

What a shame, Fran thought, to waste my new face like this. If only Debbie could see me now!

She lingered as long as she could. Then she started dabbing on cream. At a sound, she looked up, and her glance met Veronica's. Veronica smiled. In that moment Fran knew . . . knew why Veronica's face had seemed familiar. She had seen her on TV! Veronica was the girl in the breakfast-food commercial!

10

Acting Is Not Easy

"THE NAME OF THE PLAY," Roxie said the next Monday, "is, *Go, Go Ghost.*" She waited for the *ohs* and *ahs* to subside. "I thought that would please you," she said. "This class doesn't seem quite the type for fairy-tale plays."

"Is it really spooky?" Cindy asked.

"If it's done right. It ought to end the evening with a wallop. As I told you before, there will be seven plays all in the same evening, and as the oldest group, you'll be last. So you'd better be good."

Roxie sat on the edge of the table and picked up the top copy from a stack of scripts. "The story, briefly, is this: There's an old haunted house in this town. A group of teen-age girls have a club and they decide to hold a meeting in the haunted house. The two girls who are new members have to agree to stay there all night. So a couple of brothers of the girls decide to scare them by pretending to be ghosts. But unknown to everyone, there's an old lady living in the gate-house. She creeps into the haunted house to see what's going on and scares the daylights out of all of them. That's the basic idea. Okay, let's pass out the scripts and start reading."

Veronica whispered to Fran, "Sounds like this play was made to order for Andrew and Harold."

"Mmm," Fran murmured. At this moment she was too excited at the thought of playing a teen-age girl to worry about the boys.

"Who would like to begin by reading the part of the president of the girls' club?" Roxie asked. "All right, Rita. Sally, you be her best friend."

"Type casting," Veronica muttered.

Fran nodded. That must mean they were playing parts like themselves.

"Now for the other girls." Roxie paused. "Claire, you be Carol, Veronica be Betty, and Susan, Judy. Start at the beginning of the play."

The girls moved to the front of the room.

"With an air of bravery, to impress the other girls. . . ." Rita began.

"You don't read the stage directions," Roxie interrupted. "Just say the speeches."

"Oh." Rita wrinkled her forehead in cute bewilderment as Sally helpfully pointed out the correct passage.

"Any time," Roxie said with a sigh.

"See," Rita read, "it's just an old house."

"Yes, just an old haunted house," Sally read. "There's nothing to be afraid of, not really. She shudders." Sally covered her mouth. "I wasn't supposed to say that last part."

"Continue," Roxie said.

As the girls read the next three pages, Fran alternately watched the script and the players. Veronica had only one speech.

"Thank you," Roxie said suddenly. "Let's try that same scene with another group. Fran, you be the president and Nancy her best friend." She called other names.

"Give it punch," Veronica advised as Fran passed her. Rita, following, gave Fran a cold stare. Why, she wants the part of president, Fran thought.

"See," Fran read, conscious of Rita's hostile look, "it's just an old house."

"Speak up," Roxie said. "Say it with an air of confidence. This is a girl who's very sure of herself."

"See," Fran said. To her horror, the word came out with a shout. She lowered her tone abruptly for "it's just an old house."

"Could you keep your voice on a more even keel?" Roxie said. "Go on, Nancy."

As Nancy read, Fran didn't lift her eyes from the page. She knew Rita and her crowd were snickering. She tried to concentrate on a brave voice, but it came out wavering each time. At the end of the scene she returned to her seat, eyes downcast. If she could only sneak from the room!

"We'll go through the scene once more and then we'll move on," Roxie said. She chose another set of girls, this time with Claire as president.

Veronica whispered to Fran, "Boy, I wouldn't belong to a club if she were in charge."

Fran nodded, but she knew even Claire was better than she had been. The scene ended and the girls sat down.

"Okay, boys!" Roxie called.

Andrew and Harold jumped, and the scripts they had been balancing on their heads fell to the floor.

"In view of your *intense* interest," Roxie said, as they sheepishly picked up the books, "I'm going to ask you to read now. The parts of the boys in this play were tailor-made for you. It should be a real blast.

Veronica, I want you to read the part of the eccentric old woman. She's very spooky in this section. It isn't until the end of the play that she becomes a nice old thing."

Andrew and Harold took their own sweet time about getting started, and when they did read, they made it sound about as exciting as the label on a jar of olives. They aren't funny, Fran thought. They're just boring. Still, they were sure to get parts. While she, who just had to be in the play . . .

"What are you doing in my house?" Fran jerked to attention and both boys jumped as Veronica shrieked the line. This was even spookier than her witch voice.

"Wh . . . why we just happened to wander in," Andrew read. For the first time, he sounded convincing.

"Then wander OUT!" Veronica intoned. Andrew looked as though he'd like to wander right out of the building.

"Watch the book," Roxie shouted. "Keep it moving, boys." After two more pages, she released them.

"Obviously," Roxie said, "the boys will play these parts. Is there anyone else who would like to read for the old woman?" She looked around, but the girls pretended to be absorbed in their scripts. "It may not be glamorous, but it's the meatiest part in the play," Roxie urged. She shrugged, and smiled at Veronica.

"No contenders. The part is yours. I know you'll do a terrific job."

The class applauded and Veronica's face flushed with pleasure.

Roxie moved to the front of the room and checked her script against the names on the clipboard. Her eyes skimmed over the class. "Okay," she said finally. "I've got the rest set."

Fran held her breath. The whole room was hushed. "The part of president" — Roxie looked back at her notes — "will be Rita." There was an exhaling of disappointed breath, and one little squeal . . . from Rita.

"Sally." Sally looked at Roxie expectantly. "You'll be Rita's best friend." The two girls hugged each other and gave more excited squeals.

"For the rest. . . ." Roxie read down a list, calling the names of the girls and the parts they would play. Fran's name wasn't mentioned.

"Come get your playbooks before you leave," Roxie said. "And underline your speeches before the next class."

"I'll wait outside," Fran whispered to Veronica, and hurried out to the hall. She knew she had read badly. After the first awful shout, her voice had trembled. But couldn't Roxie have trusted her with a small part, with one line, even? she thought. Even just to be on stage. How humiliating it was, not to be wanted at all!

"Hey, Fran, Roxie wants you," Veronica said, as she walked out to the hall, reading the script as she went.

I guess, Fran thought, she wants me to be prop girl or something. Well, I won't do it. But she made her way back in, through the noisy class. She had to be a good sport, even though she felt like hiding somewhere and crying.

"Why did you rush off?" Roxie asked. "You forgot your script." She held out the book.

"Why . . . why do I need it?"

Roxie frowned. "To learn your lines, of course."

Fran stared in bewilderment. "Lines?"

"For Connie." Now Roxie stared, and then she rolled her eyes upward. "Don't tell me I skipped over your name."

Fran bit her lips.

Roxie looked at her list. "I must have. Sorry, Fran. You and Nancy are the girls who are being initiated into the club. Real good parts. You do a lot of screaming and carrying on. You'll be good, I know it." She took another script. "Here, run and take Nancy hers, too, will you? I just skipped over those two names."

"Thanks." Fran raced from the room, her heart pounding with joy.

Veronica, who had waited for her, helped her catch up with Nancy.

"I can't believe it! Oh, thanks, Fran!" Nancy's gentle eyes glowed.

"And the best club girls' parts," Veronica said.

"Oh? How about the part of the president of the club?" Fran asked.

"Ugh. That doesn't call for anything special. You girls get to cut loose a little."

Maybe so, Fran thought, but the club girls would look better. They didn't have to wear old clothes and crawl into sleeping bags.

"Roxie says we're going to block next week," Veronica said, twirling around. "Boy, that's when the action starts."

"Just thinking about it makes me scared!" Nancy said.

Fran gave a happy laugh. "After tryouts, I don't think anything could be too bad. . . . YIKES!"

She screamed again as something clawed at her shoulders and gave a terrible growl. Then she whirled and saw what it was.

"Andrew Willis! What's the big idea!" she shouted, now more furious than afraid.

Andrew extended his arms, fingers bent grotesquely, and lurched forward in imitation of a TV monster. "Just getting in practice," he moaned, "to scare little girls."

His shadow, Harold, picked up the action. "Little sissy girls," he imitated.

"Why don't you crawl back to your kennel?" Veronica suggested. "You look like a sick dog." She stuck out her foot to trip Harold, but he only stumbled.

"Aw, come on," Andrew said. "We'll fix them good, in the play. Then we'll see who looks sick."

"Run home and take another Stupid Pill," Veronica shouted after the running figures, "before this one wears off." She rolled her script into spyglass shape and peered after them.

"Why did they act like that, just now?" Nancy asked, looking confused.

"Because they're rotten, that's why," Veronica answered.

Fran shivered. "Hard telling what mean things they'll do backstage, when Roxie can't see them."

Nancy's big brown eyes looked puzzled. "I know Andrew acts up in class sometimes. But he's different at home. He's not mean at all. His mother calls him her little man."

Veronica lowered the tube and looked curiously at Nancy. "How do you know?" she asked.

"They live down the street from us. His mother and mine get together for coffee sometimes."

They had reached the corner where Nancy turned.

"If I didn't know better," Veronica said, "I'd say you were talking of a different Andrew. He may be a little man at home, but he's a monster on the streets."

Nancy smiled. "He's always been nice to me. I mean, he ignores me. Well, see you Thursday." She hesitated. "Fran," she murmured shyly, "I'm glad we're friends in the play."

On Thursday, the class sat as usual on folding chairs in front of the small stage. As the character they were playing entered the scene, they were to go up, come in the correct door and find their first position on stage. Everyone had to have a pencil and mark his script as he went along so at the next rehearsal he'd know what to do.

"That's right, Fran and Nancy," Roxie called as the girls entered. "Stop at that spot and give your first lines. Mark it."

As Fran was printing LC in the margin to indicate left center, she had a creepy feeling. She looked up, smack into the eyes of Andrew and Harold. They were sitting in the front row, arms folded like patriots in a history book. They were staring straight ahead . . . at her. She lowered her eyes and then in spite of herself, glanced up again. The boys continued to stare, with no expression on their faces.

Fran tried to concentrate on the scene, but she was aware of those steady looks. She began losing her place.

"Come on, Fran, get with it," Roxie said impatiently.

Fran kept her eyes on her book. She felt as though the whole world were staring at her. It was a relief when the scene moved on and the boys had to take their turn on stage.

Some time later, Fran and Nancy stood in the wings, ready to enter once more. The boys had finished their scene and were nowhere in sight. Suddenly, just as she heard her cue, Fran felt a body on one side of her and then on the other. It was the boys, stiff, and silent. Closer and closer they pressed. Finally, Fran was forced to step backward to let them move together in front of her.

Just at that moment, Nancy made her entrance on stage, expecting Fran to follow. Fran couldn't get around the boys.

"Connie, where are you?" Roxie demanded. Connie was the name of the girl Fran was playing. Fran struggled around Harold and pushed her way through the curtains.

"You'll have to watch your cues better than that," Roxie warned. "If you're late making an entrance, you'll slow down the play. Besides, it looks bad." Fran felt her face go red. She knew that was what the boys wanted, to make her look bad. But she wouldn't give them the satisfaction of letting them know she cared.

"I wish I could get my hands on them. *Pow!*" Veronica said later. "But they haven't tried anything on stage when I've been around. Don't they bother Nancy at all?"

"Not a bit. They keep out of her sight. I guess it's because she lives so close to Andrew."

After two more weeks of rehearsals, even Nancy noticed what the boys were up to. "I really believe Harold eggs Andrew on," she said. "But Andrew knows better. Should I speak to his mother about it, Fran?"

"Yikes, no!" she said. "That would only make it worse."

"At least," Nancy consoled, "you know your lines. Once you get on stage, they can't bother you."

Fran was one of the few who didn't mind the day

Roxie said, "Okay, no scripts on stage today." Groans sounded.

"Sorry," Roxie said with a grim smile that showed she wasn't sorry at all. "Dress rehearsal is coming up in five more sessions. You can't concentrate on character if you're reading from a playbook. So far," she continued, "you people don't react on stage. You show no emotion."

"How do you show emotion?" Claire wanted to know.

"By feeling it. Suppose you're happy. What do you do, just paste a big grin on your face?" The cast laughed. "If you do, you're not going to convince anyone. You have to feel happy. Or, take this play. There's a lot of fear involved. Well, we all know you're not afraid of each other."

Fran didn't dare look at the boys.

"So," Roxie said, "try to think instead, of something that really frightens you . . . and let that show in your face and in your voice. Okay. Enough talk. Let's run through the play."

A little while later, while the club girls were doing their first lines on stage, Fran stood offstage, with Nancy in front of her. Just as they were ready to go on, Harold whispered, "Hey, Andrew, you got that firecracker ready?"

"Just about," Andrew said.

Nancy entered. Fran followed, glancing nervously over her shoulder. She said her lines with a shaking voice and she kept close to Nancy for comfort. Would those boys dare throw the firecracker right in front of her?

After a while, she realized there had been no firecracker at all. It was just another trick.

At the end of the scene, Roxie called out, "That's what I meant by showing emotion. You really looked scared, Connie."

I was, Fran thought. Now she knew the meaning of that saying, "You have to suffer for your art."

11

Cobwebs and Hair Spray

ON FRIDAY, one week before the play, Fran was just about to leave the house for Nancy's to work on props when Debbie's mother called.

"Debbie will be home next Wednesday," Mrs. Wright said, "and I'm planning a slumber party for her that night. I hope you can come."

"I'd love to," Fran said, feeling a little pang of guilt because she had forgotten the day of Debbie's homecoming. "What time will it be, Mrs. Wright?"

"About seven-thirty. But why don't you come over in the afternoon? You can go with me to the station to meet her. Oh, and could you bring a sleeping bag, Frances?"

"Sure." She had never needed one before, at Debbie's. "I had to get one for the play, and I can bring it along."

"Play?" Mrs. Wright sounded vague. "You're in a play?"

It seemed odd that Fran hadn't seen Debbie's mother all summer. "Yes, it's a Park District project, but we're going to do it at the high school. I hope Debbie can come. And you too," she added politely.

"Oh, Debbie won't want to miss it," Mrs. Wright said. She didn't sound so sure about herself. "Our little grandchild is due any day now, so . . ." Mrs. Wright's voice faded and then became stronger with, "We'll see you Wednesday, then, dear."

Fran felt elated as she rushed from the house and headed for Nancy's. Next Wednesday, a slumber party. Thursday, dress rehearsal. Friday, relatives over for dinner and the play. And this was supposed to have been a dull summer!

In spite of her rush, when she spotted an old chalked hopscotch game on the sidewalk she jumped through the spaces. Her sneakers made a *whish* sound against the concrete.

Three blocks farther when she entered enemy territory—Andrew's neighborhood—she looked around warily. He wasn't in sight.

"You're just in time," Veronica announced when Fran joined the girls on the patio. "We're making cobwebs."

"Eek," Fran moaned. "Out of what?"

"Heavy twine, spray starch, ashes," Veronica said. "You should have worn older clothes. You're going to get all messed up."

"I'll do the messy part for you," Nancy said. "I don't mind. How do we start, Veronica?"

Veronica looked perplexed, but only for a moment. "Make a circle out of twine, then bigger ones. Lay them out in the design, and then knot the circles together with long pieces of twine."

"What's the spray starch for?" Fran wanted to know.

"To make it stiff. And the ashes are to make it gray and spooky-looking," Veronica said. She sat back on her heels. "Does this look big enough to you?"

"I guess so," Fran said. "We don't have to have spiders, do we?" Even the plastic ones Chip made in molds gave her the creeps.

"Andrew's going to bring some big hairy ones that look worse than real," Nancy said. "His mother says he has them hanging from the ceiling in his room."

"He would have," Veronica commented. "Hey, we forgot to lay down newspapers. What shall we

do, move this web over to the grass? Can we spray it there?"

"Sure," Nancy said.

They moved the web. Fran began spraying. The summer breeze blew the starch right across to Nancy's legs. "Hey," she said, "that's cold. And when it dries, I'll have stiff knees."

"I'll hold it closer and cup my hand around it."

"We'd better start strewing this stuff," Veronica said, bringing over a coffee can filled to the brim with ashes. "Your family must smoke a lot."

"Oh, those are from a campfire," Nancy explained. "My brother saved them for me."

The word *campfire* reminded Fran of Debbie. "Did you know Debbie's coming back next week?" she asked.

"Who's she?" Veronica wanted to know.

"My best . . . a friend of mine," Fran stammered. Nancy was looking down at her hands. "Don't you remember her? She's in our room."

"Nope," Veronica said.

"She's very popular," Nancy said timidly. "And very pretty. She has long dark hair and big blue eyes with thick lashes."

"Well, I didn't notice," Veronica said briskly. "Now, shall we sprinkle these ashes? Stand back, everybody."

The gray dust sifted gently to the make-believe web, and fell to the grass or blew away. "It isn't going to stick," Veronica said, looking piqued. "What'll we do?"

"Glue it on?" Nancy ventured, giggling.

"I don't suppose, Nancy," Veronica said, after a moment, "that your mother has any old hair spray?"

"She doesn't use it."

"Hmm." Veronica wiped her hands on the side of her jeans in a businesslike way. "Could I use your phone, then, to call my mother?"

Veronica came out of the house beaming. "All set," she said. "Mom gets lots of samples at the cosmetic counter from salesmen, and she said we could spray and ash in our garage next Wednesday afternoon. But she suggested we lower the webs into shallow pans of regular starch solution, then drag them through ashes, and use the hair spray to make it stick."

Fran laughed. "I'll bet those hair-spray people never knew their product would be used for cobwebs."

"I can just see it on TV," Veronica said. "Ladies, are the cobwebs in your house limp and straggly-looking? Then perk them up with Lady Macbeth Hair Spray."

Fran piped up with, "Witches everywhere recommend it. Mmm — it's yummy!" She didn't know why she said those last words, the words in that cereal commercial. They just slipped out. She darted a glance at Veronica. Veronica was giving her a strange look. Then she grinned. Fran grinned back.

"When did you find out?" Veronica asked.

Fran felt herself blushing, although she didn't know why. Perhaps because she had discovered something Veronica had wanted to keep secret. "I recognized you in make-up class that day, when your bangs were pulled back and you didn't have on your glasses."

"Recognized?" Nancy stared at them in bewilderment.

"Aw, I did a TV commercial out in Hollywood. My grandma Alice arranged it. It was about some crummy cereal."

"No kidding!" Nancy's eyes were round with wonder. "How exciting!"

"Exciting! Are you kidding?" Veronica pulled her fingers through her bangs. "It was a bore. I had to keep on saying, 'Mmm — it's yummy!' All day under hot lights until a dozen people were satisfied. It wasn't exciting and it wasn't acting."

"But . . ." Fran objected, "you were a star."

"Don't fool yourself," Veronica said. "That box of cereal was the star. Now, about these cobwebs . . . *girls!*"

With an effort, the two girls returned their attention

to the job at hand. Nancy frowned. "Do you think we should let all that work go until next week?" she asked. "It seems kind of risky."

"We'll have to," Veronica said. "My dad is not about to step around cobwebs on the garage floor for a week. Besides, they might get damaged. We can make them now, but the finishing touches will just have to wait until Wednesday."

Wednesday. That was the day of the slumber party. "Could we do it Thursday morning, instead?" Fran asked.

"I'm afraid they wouldn't dry in time," Veronica replied. "Why?" she said, with a sudden look at Fran. "Can't you make it Wednesday?"

"No, I . . . it's . . ." Now, why couldn't she say she had plans that involved only Debbie? There was nothing wrong with it. But her guilt was from other times. Times when she and Debbie could easily have included other girls, girls like Nancy. It had come back to her lately, how Nancy had sometimes smiled eagerly at them and they had only smiled, waved casually, and gone off. On the day of tryouts when Nancy had said, "I'm glad we're friends in the play," she might have added, "at least."

"I'm sorry," Fran murmured. She meant for everything.

"That's all right," Nancy said, as though she understood what Fran was trying to say. She turned to Veronica. "It won't take long. The two of us can surely finish the webs. Tying them is the hard part."

"Right," Veronica agreed. "Let's do two or three more. Then I'll have the rest of the week to conjure up my costume." She cut another length of twine and knotted it into a circle.

"What are you going to wear?" Nancy asked. "One of your mother's old dresses?"

"You haven't met my mother," Veronica said, with a quick smile at Fran. "No, I'm putting something together from old costumes. I'm experimenting with make-up, too, to get something really weird-o. Wouldn't it be neat if I could sneak backstage Friday and not let the boys see me before I spring out? I'd like to give them a good jolt."

"They deserve it," Fran said forcefully, "after the way they've been carrying on."

Nancy finished a knot. "Doesn't it seem, though, that Andrew has settled down lately?"

Veronica leaned back on her heels. "Come to think of it," she said, "he has. Just this week. Don't you think so, Fran?"

"I guess so," she said grudgingly. "But that doesn't mean anything. He's probably saving up for something terrible."

"I wonder," Veronica said. "But you know, another strange thing is, he knows his lines. Harold doesn't, but Andrew has them down pat."

"Oh, he's scared," Nancy said. "He doesn't want to make a fool of himself. If there's one thing Andrew can't stand, it's to have people laugh at him."

Fran's eyebrows shot up. "Oh? He did plenty of things in class to make people laugh."

Nancy frowned. "But he *wanted* them to, then. In the play, he may want to make people laugh, but not at him."

"I see what you mean," Veronica said. "There's a difference."

"That doesn't help me any," Fran observed. "He may be memorizing his lines just so he can concentrate on ruining my part."

"I wouldn't worry," Nancy said consolingly. "He'll behave. His mother will be there. So that means he'll act like a regular little gentleman."

"That," Veronica said, "may be the greatest acting of the evening."

12
Debbie Returns

THE NEXT WEDNESDAY, at the train station, Fran and Mrs. Wright walked along next to the cars of the train just in from Wisconsin. "I imagine the camp car is the last one," Mrs. Wright observed, "and no doubt the noisiest."

Her words proved true. Beyond the passengers in their summer clothes, hurrying toward the station, there came a whooping and shouting as duffle bags poured out of the last set of sliding doors, followed by a mad scramble of tanned, energetic young forms. Fran, in a rose-printed dress with matching flat-heeled shoes, felt like a visitor from another planet.

"My word, they all look alike," Mrs. Wright said,

peering through the windows at the jostling girls. Other parents, also gazing, looked equally bewildered. "Sally!" "Candy!" "Patricia!" they were calling.

"Mom!"

A tall, tanned girl hurled herself at Mrs. Wright. "Am I glad to see you!"

Fran stared at the girl with long braids who was hugging and kissing Mrs. Wright. She looked like a blue-eyed Pocahontas.

"Fran!" Debbie let go of her mother to give Fran a bear hug. "It's really neat-o of you to come meet me." She stepped backward, still holding her friend's arms. "You look different. Really neat-o! Hey, Goons!" she called, suddenly whirling. Two girls across the noisy crowd detached themselves from their parents and baggage to wave frantically at Debbie. One stuck two fingers in her mouth and gave a shrill whistle. "See you tonight!" Debbie called.

"What?" One girl screamed over the noise. Fran recognized her as Shirley, from her room at school.

"Tonight!" Debbie yelled, cupping her hands like a megaphone around her mouth. "At my house."

Shirley nodded, and shrugged, pointing toward her mother's back.

Debbie said, "She isn't sure her mother will want her to go away the first night back, but she's going to

work on it." She giggled. "She'll manage, if I know Shirley. You should have seen how she got around the counselors at camp."

"Hmm," Mrs. Wright said, looking a little displeased. "Can we collect your luggage and get out of here?"

Shirley did manage, and so did Rosemary. They had been Debbie's cabin mates, along with three other girls. They seemed a little annoyed that Fran was included in the homecoming party, but after a bit they ignored her.

That night when they were sitting around on the patio there was an endless parade of remember-whens. For a while Fran listened in. Then her mind began to wander.

She reached out and caught a lightning bug, watched it glow once and wing away. The bug reminded her of Chip. He still hadn't bought his Alamo game. He seemed to be short of money again, but she didn't know just why.

". . . been doing all summer?" She heard Debbie's words and in the silence, realized they had been spoken to her.

"Oh." She fumbled. "Fooling around. And of course," she continued, as three faces looked at her, "there were drama classes." She tried to get excitement into her voice. "We're doing the play Friday."

"Oh?" Shirley paused for a yawn. "They had some kind of acting at camp, but hardly anyone was interested."

"Well, I would have been," Debbie said, with a glance at Fran, "only I didn't want to do it by myself."

"I'm sleepy," Rosemary said. "I can't take these late hours." For some reason, this prompted wild laughter from the three of them.

"It must be eight o'clock at least," Rosemary continued. "Practically the dead of night." Fran half smiled as they laughed again, but she couldn't help thinking that camp had made them a little childish.

Debbie turned in explanation. "We had to have lights out by eight," she said. "But no one settled down for hours."

"Except when the counselors came by to check," Shirley added.

"What time did you get up?" Fran asked, just to be polite.

"Eck! Don't mention it!" Shirley and Rosemary outdid each other in squealing now. "Practically at daybreak!" "And we had to take a dip in the lake before breakfast!" "I'm going to sleep until noon tomorrow."

I can't, Fran thought. I have to go over and help check on the spiderwebs. She and Nancy were going to meet with Veronica to be sure everything was ready to go.

In spite of their protests that they never *really* went to sleep until midnight, Shirley and Rosemary, in their sleeping bags, were soon breathing deeply. Fran, nearest the wall, heard Debbie stir in the sleeping bag next to her.

"You awake?" Debbie whispered.

"Yes. Aren't you tired?"

"Sure, but I'm too excited to sleep." Debbie's hair made a soft swish on the pillowcase as she tossed her hair in the darkness. "Being back in my own room again, and seeing everybody. Everything seems so different. You know . . ." She paused. "You seem different too."

"Me? How?" Fran couldn't see Debbie's eyes in the shadows.

Debbie hesitated. "I don't know. Just different." There was a longer pause and a rustling as she plumped up her pillow. "Who all is going to be in the play? Not Andrew Willis, I hope." She gave a groan. "Boy, would he spoil it!"

"Yeah, he's in it," Fran said. "So is Veronica."

"She is? Does she still go around saying 'I'm from

Hollywood, the glamour capital of the world?' " Debbie asked, with disgust in her voice.

"No. She's really . . . neat-o," Fran said, borrowing Debbie's term. And before Debbie could reply, she added, "She's the best actress in class, and — "

One of the sleeping girls moaned and flung a hand . . . *thump* . . . on the carpet. "Shut up," she said sleepily.

Debbie giggled softly. "I guess she wants us to shut up. When is the play, again?" she whispered.

"Friday night."

"I'll be there. That is," she added glumly, "if my sister's baby doesn't decide to get born that day. It isn't even here yet, and its running my life already."

"It is?"

"Sure, that's the main reason I was sent to camp all summer. So Mother could rest up. And help my sister get ready."

They were silent a few moments. "Don't you want a baby in the family?" Fran asked softly.

Debbie hesitated. "I don't care. It's just . . ." Her voice broke. "I've always been the youngest."

"I know."

"I guess . . . " Debbie paused for an exhausted yawn. "I'll go to sleep now. I'm awfully tired."

"Me too." But Fran lay for a long time in the darkness, thinking.

Habit, perhaps, made the girls wake up fairly early. No one lingered over breakfast. Now that the party was over, Rosemary and Shirley seemed eager to go home and see what had been happening all summer. Debbie was slated to go with her mother on errands, one of which was to have her hair cut. "Want to come along?" Debbie asked Fran.

"No, thanks. I have . . . things to do." Fran didn't want to go into details about the spiderwebs. It was too complicated. "Remember, save tomorrow night," she said. "The plays start at seven-thirty, in the high school."

"Plays?"

"All the kids in drama class have to do one. Ours is last."

"I'll bet you're scared," Debbie said.

And with those words, Fran felt the first little stabbings of fear right in her middle. It wasn't a daydream. She really was going to get up on a stage, with lights blazing on her, saying lines in front of a lot of strangers. But even worse than strangers was the thought of family and friends, who would be watching her every move.

13

A Dreadful Dress Rehearsal

"THEY TURNED OUT super!" Veronica said, holding up a web, as Fran entered the garage later that morning. "See, nice and stiff."

"And spooky," Nancy added. "All they need is the spiders."

At the word *spiders*, Fran shuddered. "I hope they're not too crawly-looking."

"The creepier, the better," Veronica said matter-of-factly. "Listen, we have to do everything we can to make the play scary. If the audience once starts laughing, we're sunk."

Fran said a little crossly, "I still think the boys are going to try to make the audience laugh." Before

Nancy could defend Andrew, she added, "Don't tell me Harold is afraid of Mrs. Willis, too."

"No, but he's afraid of Andrew."

"How are we going to get all this stuff over to the school tonight?" Veronica asked. "Could your mother take us in the station wagon, Fran?"

"She said she would. I have to take that little table, too, so we'll pick you up on the way. Let's go early so we can watch some of the other plays. Okay?"

They all agreed that was a good idea. Roxie had said that on Friday night everyone would have to wait out in the hall.

When they entered the darkened theatre, a group of small children was practicing on stage. From the looks of their costumes, and the paper petals framing their faces, Fran guessed they were flowers in some nursery garden.

"Where should we put the things?" whispered Mrs. Sanders, who had helped carry in the props.

"Here in the side aisle, I guess," Veronica whispered back. "We'll sit here and guard them."

"Aren't they adorable?" Mrs. Sanders said, looking at the children on stage. "The yellow one, the sun-flower, looks like the little Appleton girl."

The door at the back of the auditorium kept open-ing to let children in. They were wearing costumes, or parts of costumes, and carrying everything from tree branches stuck in buckets to doll beds. Children streamed up and down the aisles and back and forth, banging seats as they went. Roxie, up front, seemed not to notice.

"She must have nerves of steel," Mrs. Sanders said, shaking her head. "I'll see you girls later." Daylight entered as she opened the door. Other girls from Fran's group came over to join them. Like Fran and Nancy, they were in the sports clothes they would wear in the play.

"Where's your costume, Veronica?" one of them asked.

"Here," Veronica said, patting a long clothes box. "I'll change later, in the washroom."

"Curtain!" Roxie called.

The flowers wiggled and waved to friends in the audience as the curtains closed.

"Open!" Roxie yelled.

As the flowers were once more revealed, Roxie said loudly, "Be here tomorrow night at seven in full make-up and costume. I'll have signs in the hall with the names of the plays. Gather at yours, and no running around. All right, cast for *Sleeping Beauty* on stage left, and prop people set the stage. You have the cradle? Okay, a doll bed will do. The rest of you people out there, keep quiet."

Rita and Sally came down the center aisle. When

their eyes had adjusted to the darkness, they scooted across the folded seats to join the *Ghost* group. Both girls wore brand new dresses. Rita had her forward curls taped to her cheeks.

"I thought we were all going to wear sports clothes," Claire said accusingly.

"Well, wouldn't the president of a club — " Rita said with a smirk. "I mean . . ."

"I don't see why she would," Claire persisted. "It isn't as though — "

"Shh," Veronica hissed. "Give the kids on stage a break." She leaned forward and rested her elbows on the back of the seat.

"Yeah," said a boy's voice on the other side of Fran. "Give the kids a break."

Fran looked toward the darkened side aisle. She could just barely make out the faces of Andrew and Harold.

"Watch out for the props," someone cautioned.

At that moment Harold stumbled. "Now you tell us," he said.

On stage, while the good fairies wrung their hands and looked unhappy, the bad fairy was telling the king and queen that their baby daughter would prick her finger on a spindle at the age of sixteen and die. The king, a stocky boy of about nine, had the hiccups.

After the last good fairy said, "She will not die, but will sleep for a hundred years," the curtains closed swiftly.

"Okay, set up for scene two," Roxie called.

She strolled up the aisle, clipboard in hand, checking off names. "Everybody in the *Ghost* cast here?" she asked, stopping at Fran's group. "Good, you can go on after *Sleeping Beauty*."

"Are we going to have the spooky lighting today?" Andrew asked.

"Absolutely. Everything but make-up. Did you boys bring the iron chain you're supposed to drag?"

"Yep. And the green flashlights."

"Okay. You people can slip out to the hall and get your stuff ready to go on." She turned and advanced toward the stage. "Are you ready up there? You'll have to change sets faster than that, or the audience will fall asleep. Let's go. Curtain!"

Fran and Veronica moved to the side aisle where their props were stored. Nancy followed. "We'll have to make two trips," Veronica said. "Easy with the webs."

"We'll carry them," Nancy said. "You have your costume and lantern."

Harold scrunched forward. "I'll carry your sleeping bag, Fran," he said.

Fran stared.

Harold knelt and started to lift a rolled-up bag. "This yours?" he asked.

"No, that one."

He dropped Nancy's and picked up the bag Fran had pointed out.

"What's the difference?" Andrew said. "Just grab one."

Harold, however, bundled Fran's bag under his arm, and with his free hand picked up his chain and folded costume. His flashlight was stuck in his hip pocket.

Andrew took Nancy's bag. "Wait for me," he hissed, but Harold was already out in the hall.

"Could that be our own dear boys? Such gentlemen," Doreen said, echoing Fran's thoughts.

"You notice they didn't take the table," Susan said. "Come on, Doreen, we can carry it."

The girls, with lanterns, boxes, webs, and table, made their way down the hall.

"Watch it, please," Fran said to some children playing tag. "Don't bump into us."

"You little kids had better get back inside," Doreen said. "And pipe down."

The children, cardboard wings flapping, ran down the hall, banging their fists on metal lockers.

Veronica disappeared into the washroom, costume box in hand. The boys, with their sheets, likewise disappeared.

"I'll see if *Sleeping Beauty* is almost over," Sally volunteered. Just then the cast came streaming out. The king was still hiccuping.

Roxie appeared. "Tomorrow night," she said to the *Ghost* group, "you'll follow a play called *The Whistler's Song*. As soon as they clear the stage, set your scene. I'll have two boys working lights and curtains, so you won't have to worry about that. You can go in now, and get set."

Nancy took hold of Fran's arm. "Are you nervous?"

"A little."

"Me, too. And it's only dress rehearsal. Got your flashlight?"

"Yes," Fran said. It was slippery in her moist hand. They picked up their sleeping bags where the boys had dumped them and carried them onto the wing on stage left. It was a bigger stage than the one at the park building.

On stage, Fran saw the prop committee placing the odds and ends of beat-up furniture and hanging the webs. She could hardly bear to look at the huge, hairy spiders that dangled from strings. One of the girls was pinning an old torn net curtain over the doorway.

In a sort of cage, just left of the stage, a boy was pulling different switches. As he did so, the lights on the stage changed from bright to dim and from blue to red. He had a spotlight placed to shine where she and Nancy would lie in their sleeping bags.

Fran and Nancy clung to each other. Everything was so exciting. And frightening.

The door leading to the hall opened. Something in black came in. It wore a tattered rustly black dress, black laced pointed shoes, and a slouch hat over straggly gray hair. It carried a lantern. Veronica!

"How do I look, girlies?" she asked, in a quavering, moaning sort of voice.

"Eek!" Fran and Nancy giggled, drawing instinctively away from her.

"You keep away from my house . . . hear?" Veronica threatened.

"Gladly," Fran said.

There was a thump and bump as the boys, wrapped in sheets, followed.

"Watch it," one of them said. "You're walking on my sheet. I may have to sleep on it next week."

Roxie strolled over. "If you can't cut eye-holes in the sheets, you'll have to make head coverings of white paper bags. You boys have to be completely disguised so the girls are really frightened."

"They will be anyway," one of them said, and snickered.

"Places, everyone!" called Roxie. "Give it everything you've got. I'm going to be out front watching, and I want to feel cold chills up and down my spine. Break a leg!"

"Huh?" several people said.

"That's stage talk. It's considered bad luck to say 'Good luck.' So instead, you say, 'Break a leg.'" Roxie grinned. "Now don't take me literally. You boys hitch up those sheets a little."

She turned to the bored teenager stationed to pull curtains. "Mike, just give me a chance to get out front, and then begin." In a few moments, her voice called, "Curtain!" and from the wings Fran could see the light from the stage pouring out over the first few rows of seats.

The girls' club entered the stage, laughing and talking, and then came the familiar lines:

"See, it's just an old house."

"Yes, just an old haunted house. There's nothing to be afraid of, not really."

Fran, trembling, awaiting her cue, thought, No, there's nothing to be afraid of, so I wish I could stop shaking.

The time came closer for her entrance. Her legs felt

156

as though there were no bones in them. Her hands, now, instead of being moist, were stiff and cold.

Nancy gripped her arm. "I'm scared."

"Me too. Well, here we go." With flashlights and sleeping bags they entered the white, hot light of the stage. Dust motes danced in front of Fran's eyes. She was conscious of the children scattered in the seats out front. A toddler, walking along the front row, was banging down all the seats. Fran forced her attention to the people on stage.

"You'll be surprised." She said her line as she had rehearsed it many times. "When you come back in the morning, we'll be right here."

"Yes," Nancy said. "There are no such things as ghosts. Everybody knows that."

As the lines continued, Fran found it easier and easier to speak and to stroll around naturally. Being on stage wasn't so frightening. The nervous time was just before, getting ready to go on.

When the club girls left, Fran and Nancy, as Connie and Dorothy, prepared to spend the night in the haunted house. The lights gradually dimmed as they took off their shoes and unzipped the sleeping bags.

They started scooting into them. With one part of her mind, Fran heard Nancy's familiar line, "Do you really think there are things creeping around this house?" Her answer, "Don't be silly," was there, ready. But she couldn't bring it out. Her right hand had just touched something inside the bag. Something creepy. A spider! A horrible, sticky spider that seemed to clutch at her fingers. And she couldn't escape . . . or even scream . . . not on stage, with everyone looking at her! She could feel her heart thumping. Her fingers seemed paralyzed. "Don't," she stammered, and her voice sounded foreign to her, "be silly." She managed to pull her hand away from the horrible spider . . . and carefully, carefully, eased herself into the bag, keeping to one side.

"Then let's try to go to sleep," Nancy said, continuing her lines.

Somehow, Fran got through the next few speeches. When the boys entered and the two girls ran to cower in a corner, she felt safe, although she was trembling with rage. I hate him, she thought. He's mean and spiteful.

Fran and Nancy ran from the stage and in the course of the play the boys were, in turn, terrified by Veronica who circled them with her dusky lantern, moaning and chanting. I wish she'd give them a good kick! Fran thought.

"Veronica is really spooky," Nancy murmured, peering through a crack in the backstage curtains. "Spooky even without makeup!" She took Fran's hand. "Our cue's coming up."

159

They went in for the last few lines, when the mysterious goings-on were explained and the girls were assured they had earned the rights to be members of the club. Then the curtains closed.

Roxie bounded in from the hall. She moved fast.

"Nice performance," she said. "Rita, speak up a little louder on those opening lines, and boys, watch your timing on that first entrance. You were a little slow."

"My friend," Andrew said, giving Harold an angry look, "was goofing off. What was so doggoned funny?" he asked, confronting his fellow ghost.

Harold started to snicker, but subdued by Andrew's menacing look, shrugged uncomfortably. "I didn't do anything," he grumbled. His eyes, for just a second, rested on Fran. In that instant she knew it was Harold, not Andrew, who had sneaked the spider into her sleeping bag!

Roxie's look settled on Fran. "What happened to you today?" she asked. "You acted as though your sleeping bag was going to bite you. Don't hesitate like that. Keep the action moving."

Fran felt her cheeks flame, but she said nothing.

"All in all, though," Roxie said, "it was a good performance. See you at seven sharp tomorrow."

You won't see me, Fran thought. I've had enough.

Why should I get up there and let those boys make a fool of me in front of Debbie and my family and everyone? I'm quitting!

But from somewhere, Veronica's words came back. "I have to find out who I am." And who was *she*? Fran Sanders, the coward? She felt ashamed.

By the time they moved into the hall, she was furious. Why should she have to take the blame for something Harold had done?

Harold and Andrew were standing by the locker, arguing. Or rather, Andrew was talking and Harold was looking resentful. Fran started toward them.

". . . so shape up," Andrew was saying. "And learn your lines before you louse up the — " He hesitated as Fran came up.

"Another thing." Fran was even more angry. "You can just take that spider out of my sleeping bag, Harold Holbrook."

"Huh?" Andrew's mouth dropped open.

Harold tried to smile but couldn't.

"That *what?*" Veronica asked, walking up with Nancy.

"He put one of those . . . things . . . into my bag when he carried it for me." Fran's voice broke.

"Oh, for Pete's sake." Andrew gave Harold a furious look. "So that's what you thought was so funny!"

Harold shuffled. "Can't you guys take a little joke?"

"It's no joke," Veronica pronounced. "You don't play tricks on the stage."

"Heck, no," Andrew chimed in. Fran couldn't believe that he was suddenly on the girls' side. "You'll louse up the whole play!"

"Who cares!" Harold scoffed. "I didn't want to go to those dumb classes anyway. You made me do it! I didn't want to be in any play!"

Andrew backed away a little. "Well, it's too late, now. And my mother . . ."

"Your mother!" Harold jeered.

Andrew swallowed. "My mother is coming tomorrow night. And not only that — she's bringing her whole women's group!"

This sounded so strange, coming from Andrew, that Fran would have laughed, except for the odd, unhappy look on his face.

Harold glared at Andrew. "Well, nobody I know is coming, so I'm not worried one bit." He shuffled away, hands pushed into his pockets. At the corner of the hall he turned. "Don't think you're going to be so great tomorrow night," he called to Andrew. "You big jerk. You'll see!"

Andrew blinked and looked away. Then, mumbling something about getting the spider, he slipped through the stage door.

"I can't believe it," Veronica said, staring after him. "Is he really that scared of his mother?"

"Not scared," Nancy said. "It's just what I told you. He's a perfect little man around the house. That's what all the women call him."

"Boy, it's no wonder he cuts loose every place else, then," Veronica observed. "It has to come out somewhere. But doesn't his mother know how he acts in school? Doesn't she ever get called?"

"You know . . . " Fran had never thought of this before. "Andrew never does anything that bad. He teases a lot, but he always stops just before he gets into real trouble."

"Then we can consider him stopped," Veronica said. "As far as the play is concerned. Now let's hope he puts the skids on Harold."

It was almost too much to hope for, Fran thought. Harold was really angry now. But, she realized, he was angry at Andrew, not her. So there was really nothing to worry about. Was there?

14

The Day of the Play

FRAN TRIED to keep busy all day Friday because every time she let her mind leap forward to that night, when she would be on stage facing an audience, an icicle of fear stabbed her middle.

Luckily, there was plenty to do around the house. Aunt Margaret and Great-Aunt Clara were coming for a family dinner before going to the play.

"Gee, do I have to go to that boring thing?" Chip complained, leaning his elbows on the kitchen counter. He was waiting for the cake to be mixed so he could lick the beaters.

"No, you don't have to go," Mrs. Sanders said. "You can stay home alone and watch television."

"Oh, okay, I'll go," Chip said, as though he were doing them a big favor. "I can hardly wait to see Veronica." There was no pretense in his voice now. "I bet she'll be good!"

"How about your sister?" Mrs. Sanders said, turning off the mixer and lifting back the top. "Don't you think she'll be good too?"

"I suppose." Chip reached for one of the sticky beaters. "But not nearly as good as Veronica."

"Mother!" Fran wailed in protest.

"Sorry I brought it up," Mrs. Sanders said with a sigh. "Chip, when you're through with that mess, how about scrubbing some potatoes? It might clean you up at the same time. And Fran . . ."

As though on cue, the telephone rang.

". . . please answer that," Mrs. Sanders said, with a laugh. "I want to get this cake in the oven right away."

It was Debbie. "You'll never guess what!" she squealed. "Something really neat-o. I'm an aunt!"

"You are?" Fran said dumbly, bewildered by the joy in Debbie's voice.

"It happened last night," Debbie said, with a rush, "at around midnight, and he weighs close to seven pounds and he has dark hair, and his name is going to be either David or Michael, I get to help decide, and I'm going to see him in a few days when my sister goes home." She gasped for breath.

"Gosh," Fran said.

"And so, well," Debbie said, laughing, "I thought I'd call and tell you. I've got to hang up now. My mom wants to use the phone again. She's calling *everyone*. But while I have the chance . . . do you think I could go to the play with you tonight? My folks want to go to the hospital."

"Sure. Just come over. See you later, Debbie."

"Guess what," Fran said, turning from the phone. "Debbie's sister had her baby."

"Wonderful," Mrs. Sanders said. "Is it a boy or a girl?"

"A boy, and he has dark hair . . ."

"Hey, that's great," Chip interrupted. "I can teach him how to play baseball."

Mrs. Sanders rumpled his hair. "Later. How about getting at those potatoes now? Fran and I are going to set the table."

"Shall we use the good silver?" Fran asked.

"Of course. This is an occasion."

"I know," Fran said. "It will be Aunt Clara's first time out since she hurt her ankle."

Mrs. Sanders put her palms on Fran's cheeks and

kissed her lightly on the forehead. "That's one thing," she said, "but I was thinking about the play. We're all happy for you, you know."

"Except Chip," Fran said in a low voice, a little embarrassed. "He isn't happy for me."

Mrs. Sanders gave a little secret smile. "Wait," she murmured. "You may be surprised."

Yes, Fran thought, setting out the silver, I'll be surprised all right, if he behaves himself at the play. But as she worked her way around the table she had to admit, grudgingly, that Chip behaved pretty well away from home. Just the opposite, she thought, of Andrew Willis.

With Andrew came thoughts of Harold. Ugh! She could still feel that spider. She slid open a door in the buffet and got out the good plates. They began rattling as she set them on the table. She would have to think about something else. She was getting nervous again.

Later she took a long warm bath and put on her best dress, although she'd have to change again before she left for the play. As she was brushing her hair, Veronica called.

"Hey, is someone going to drive you over early tonight?" she asked. "Because my folks can't, they'll be a little late. I'd feel weird-o walking down the street with my make-up on. So I wondered if I could bring my junk to your house and get a ride?"

"Sure, my dad will drive us," Fran said. "Are you nervous?"

"Nope," Veronica said. "I hope I am before curtain time, though. You know what they say, a calm actor is a lousy actor."

"That's right," Fran agreed. She was sure it was true if Veronica said so. "Come over at about six-thirty?"

"Okay. EEEEEeeeeeee!" Veronica gave her stage shriek and hung up.

Things started happening. Aunt Margaret drove up, and as she and Mrs. Sanders were helping Great-Aunt Clara and her cane wiggle out of the car, Mr. Sanders pulled into the driveway.

"Allow me," he said, extending an arm to the relative. "She needs a man to lean on. Right, Chip?"

"Right! I'll get the door!" Chip rushed ahead.

Mrs. Sanders and Aunt Margaret and Fran waited behind, smiling as the woman in the printed voile dress hobbled forward, pausing now and then to laugh at a remark from Mr. Sanders.

"She's in such good spirits today," Aunt Margaret said, beaming. "It's doing her a world of good, getting out of the house." She tightened her arm around Fran's shoulder. "And how are your spirits today?"

"Excited," Fran said.

Great-Aunt Clara settled in a comfortable chair and caught her breath. "You know, Chip," she said, "I haven't heard news of you since the party of the year." She held her cane across her lap like the bar of a Tilt-a-Whirl and looked around the room. "House seems as usual," she observed.

"Aw." Chip ducked his head and grinned. "The damage was outside."

Great-Aunt Clara cleared her throat. "Well, as long as the house is still standing, I guess you've a closet to put it into. Your birthday present, child," she said as Chip looked at her blankly. "Long overdue, but better late than not at all. In the car. Get it," she said, as Chip stood poised. He was gone in a flash, and almost before the sound of the car door's slam reached them, he was back in the room, tearing at the astronaut-printed wrappings.

"My Alamo game!" he breathed. "At last!"

"It's overdue," Aunt Clara repeated.

"No, I mean, I've been saving for it all summer, but with one thing and another ...!" He shot a glance at his father and almost fell over his own feet, rushing toward him. He whispered excitedly in Mr. Sanders' ear.

"I sure did," Mr. Sanders said. "In the car."

Again Chip shot from the room, and again the slam came from the car door. Fran and her Aunt Margaret exchanged puzzled looks.

"What's going on?" Great-Aunt Clara asked. "Could someone please tell me?"

Chip rushed in. "Here it is!" he wheezed, thrusting a long white box at his father.

"Not to *me*," Mr. Sanders said, giving Chip a little turn. Chip stepped toward Fran and put the box into her arms.

"What is it?" she asked, startled. Her fingers trembled as she untied the white satin bow and slid the ribbon from the box. Then off came the stiff white lid, with green tissue underneath. A parting of the crinkly green, and there . . . red roses! Deep red, like velvet . . . and a fragrance that made her almost giddy. "Oh!" was all she could say.

Chip dropped to his knees beside her. "Read the card," he urged.

"*Love to Our Star,*" she read, "*from Chip, Mother, and Dad.*"

"I wanted to say, 'Break a leg,'" Chip remarked,

"but Mother wouldn't let me, on account of what almost happened to Great-Aunt Clara."

"Now, why would you say such a fool thing on a card, anyway?" Great-Aunt Clara demanded. "Break a leg!"

"It means 'Good luck' in stage talk," Chip explained. "If you say 'Good luck,' it may bring bad luck."

"Never heard of such nonsense," Great-Aunt Clara mumbled. "Fran, you'd better take up something more sensible."

"It's just part of the game," Aunt Margaret said. "No one takes it seriously. Fran, your roses are just lovely."

"They should be," Chip said. "They cost — " Mrs. Sanders clapped her hand over his mouth.

"I mean," he said, releasing himself, "I really did help pay for them, didn't I?"

"Yes, you did," Mrs. Sanders agreed.

"That was nice of you, Chip," Fran said, holding up one of the dewy roses. "Especially when you were trying to save your money for the Alamo game."

"Oh my game!" Chip pounced on it, then sprang to plant a kiss on Great-Aunt Clara's cheek.

"Child! You're going to break my jawbone!" Aunt Clara exclaimed. Still, she held Chip close until he wriggled free.

"He reminds me so of my younger brother," the old aunt reminisced, as Chip left the room with his game. "The same sweet ways, the same sweet mischief. . . ."

"Fran." Aunt Margaret held out her hand. "Shall we go put your flowers in a vase?"

Dinner was just over when Debbie arrived. She was wearing a white embroidered cotton dress which made her summer tan even more pronounced.

"You've cut your hair!" Aunt Margaret exclaimed. Her look swept from the shining, softly curled hair to the flat white pumps. "You've changed so much, Debbie, since the last time I saw you."

"She's even changed since I saw her," Fran said. And both girls laughed, remembering the disheveled Debbie that had tumbled off the camp train.

"But so grown-up," Aunt Margaret persisted. "Oh, well . . ." and she laughed. "Of course, you've become an aunt. That's an aging process." She winked at Fran. "I should know."

"You've heard about the baby," Debbie began. "Did you know — " Fran didn't stay because she heard Veronica's voice from the hall.

"Here she is!" Chip shouted. And as Fran came up, he said, "Veronica wants to see your flowers."

"I do?" Veronica asked, but went along to the dining room willingly enough.

"See? Red roses. I helped pay for them," Chip said proudly.

"Remember Debbie?" Fran asked, as the girl in white strolled into the dining room. "She's in our room at school."

"Oh," Veronica said. "So you're Debbie. Hi."

"Hello." Debbie's expression didn't change, but Fran knew she was taking in Veronica's faded, cut-off jeans and old, limp top. Veronica's hair had grown even shaggier and odder in color.

"Let's go slap on our make-up," Veronica suggested.

"Coming, Debbie?" Fran said hesitantly.

"In a minute. I want to talk to your aunt."

When they got to her room, Fran said, "She's sharp-looking, isn't she? Debbie, I mean."

"Yeah, she's okay. Listen, I brought along all kinds of gook, so let's clear off this dresser so we won't spoil anything. You're wearing straight make-up, I take it?"

"I . . . I guess so."

"Okay, help yourself. My mother really loaded me up with stuff." Veronica began laying out jars and tubes on the dresser top. "You'd better change first. You'd ruin that dress."

"Sure." Now with the excitement of getting ready, Fran didn't mind at all getting into sports clothes. She was an actress, after all, and she had to look the part.

"What are you doing?" Debbie almost squealed, coming suddenly into the room. "You mean you're wearing *that?*"

"Yep."

"Hah," Veronica said. "Wait'll she sees my get-up, eh, Fran?"

As the girls, now in costumes, began making up, Debbie sat on the bed, trying not to appear too interested. Her mouth was pulled down in disapproval, but her eyes were envious.

This was a new kind of feeling for Fran. For the first time she felt older and experienced, while Debbie seemed a little girl in a white dress, watching her elders.

Veronica smoothed brown, green, and even purple shadow above and below her eyes, making them look huge and spooky. She shaded her cheeks with brown to give them a sunken look, and aged her face with wrinkles drawn on with eyebrow pencil. "Now for the wig, heh, heh," she cackled, and snatched it from a brown paper bag.

"Ugh," Debbie said, awed in spite of herself, "you look awful."

Veronica whirled and gave her a big grin. She had blacked out two of her teeth. "Thank you, my dear," she croaked.

It was time to go. Chip, who couldn't take his eyes off Veronica, wanted to ride along with Mr. Sanders when he deposited the girls. Debbie decided she'd rather not.

"Have fun," Mrs. Sanders said, hugging Fran carefully, so as not to spoil her make-up. "You, too, Veronica. We're all looking forward to the play."

"Frances!" her great-aunt called from the living room as they started to leave.

"Yes?" She went to the doorway.

Great-Aunt Clara raised her cane above her head, as though leading a troop charge. "Break a leg!" she shouted.

Fran grinned. "Thanks, Aunt Clara." She could hardly bear it. Everyone was being so nice!

15

Curtain Time

WHEN MR. SANDERS turned the corner toward the school, they moved into a solid line of cars. Children in costumes streamed from every direction . . . elves, bunnies, kings with lopsided crowns, and an occasional flower.

"Maybe you'd better get out here," Mr. Sanders suggested. "It's getting late. I'll go home and hurry up the women or there won't even be any seats left."

Parents milled about the hall. Fran, glancing into the auditorium, saw quite a few seats filled. Again, the icicle of fear hit her. This was for real. No more rehearsals. The audience was waiting, and they would see Fran Sanders up there on that stage. She clutched her stomach. "I'm really scared now," she said.

"Me, too, thank goodness," Veronica said.

As they approached the screens that blocked off the hall leading to the stage door, they heard a mighty roar. "It sounds like feeding time at the zoo," Veronica commented.

They stepped past the screens. They were immediately knocked against the metal lockers by a boy in a dog suit chasing another boy in a clown costume.

"Watch it!" Veronica snapped. Two cowboys joined the chase while girls in flower costumes shrieked.

Although there were poster boards stuck to the walls at intervals, giving the names of plays, no one seemed to be in the right spot. The hall was a wild mixture of gypsies, kings, elves, pirates, Japanese dancers, dogs, and cowboys, roaming about, shouting, fighting, chasing, and in one or two cases, crying.

"Where's our group?" Fran shouted above the din.

The boy in the dog suit rushed by again, knocking Veronica against a fake palm tree.

"Listen, Rover," she hollered, "you do that again, and I'll bite you!"

"Where's Roxie?" Fran felt worried.

"She probably took one look and went home,"

Veronica said, settling her costume. "Hey, there's our gang. Down there at the end of the hall."

They stepped around two little girls sitting on the floor, trying on each other's shoes. By dodging, ducking and struggling, they finally reached their *Go, Go Ghost* group. "Whew, what a mess!" Veronica groaned. "There must be a hundred kids here."

"And to think we have to wait until last!" Claire said. "It isn't fair." Fran saw that instead of the blue slack suit Claire had worn for rehearsal, she was now decked out in a pink dotted organdy dress with ruffles at the neck and sleeves. Rita and Sally were looking at her with annoyance.

A blast from a whistle cut into the hall noise and another blast quieted it down to a hum.

"Okay, people," Roxie said in the near quiet, "Get to your places, under your play signs."

The noise that followed was twice as loud as the noise before. Roxie seemed calm as she talked to the teen-age boys in charge of lights and curtains. She gave another blast of the whistle.

"Charlie Thompson, I mean you too!" she called pleasantly. "Get to your place, and stay there." She walked halfway down the hall. "We'll begin in fifteen minutes," she said. She wasn't shouting, but her voice could easily be heard. Why, Fran thought, she's *projecting.* She's making her voice move out from her body, so it carries.

"I'll pass out programs," Roxie said, "so you can see where you are on the list. When the play ahead of yours is on stage, get ready. When they come out, move quietly on stage and set your props." She started for the stage door and paused. "When your play is over, you may go to the back of the auditorium and watch the other plays. But BE QUIET!"

"Oh, great," Rita said. "We'll be stuck out here all night."

"It'll go fast," Veronica said. "The evening will be over before we know it."

"I wish it were over now," Nancy said. "I'm scared."

"You'll be fine," Fran said comfortingly, "as soon as you get on stage." As she said those words, a sudden fear struck her. She hadn't thought to check her sleeping bag, and now it was too late. Could Harold have sneaked in early and deposited another spider? She glanced at the boy, leaning against a locker. So innocent-looking! And Andrew . . . why, Andrew wasn't here. He hadn't come!

She motioned to Veronica and wispered, "Andrew isn't here."

Veronica blinked without her glasses. "Hey, Harold," she called, "where's your sidekick?"

"You mean Andrew?"

"No," Veronica said sarcastically, "King Kong."

"Where's Andrew?" other cast members murmured. "What will we do if he doesn't show up?"

"Oh, he'll show up," Harold said with a little snort. "He's just chicken."

"Why should he be chicken?" Fran asked. "Just because of your threat?" She surprised herself, speaking up like that.

"The last I heard," Nancy said, "his mother is bringing at least twelve women. He probably had to go along to pick up some of them."

"Doesn't he have a father?" Veronica asked.

"Oh, yes. But he travels."

"Well, so would I," Veronica said. She hiked up her skirt and settled cross-legged on the floor. "Might as well relax," she commented. The other girls joined her, all but Rita and Sally and Claire, who couldn't wrinkle their dresses.

The noise in the hall rose again. One or two fights broke out. A cowboy hat and a pair of cardboard bunny ears lay trampled with dusty footprints.

The teen-age curtain puller came out from the stage door. "Pipe down, you guys," he called rudely, "we can't hear the actors. And the second play is supposed to be ready to go on." He scowled and disappeared inside the stage area.

"One down, and five to go," Cindy said, twisting the tail of her shirt. "It's going fast."

The first group poured out of the door, flushed and excited, with Roxie following. She patted a couple of flowers and steered them toward the exit, while urging on the next group. "Third play, get ready," she called, and went back to the stage area.

"What'll we do," Doreen asked, "if Andrew doesn't show up?"

Veronica shrugged. "Harold will have to say his lines too."

"Ho de ha ha," Harold said. "I'd leave first."

At that moment, a very nervous-looking Andrew came working his way past the costumed actors. He tried to smile, but his face was white and strained-looking beneath the sprinkling of freckles.

"You look pale," Harold said. "Pale as a ghost."

Ignoring him, Andrew came over to the girls. "Where's Roxie?" he asked. "I need someone to help me with my sheet."

"Oh, we'll do it," Veronica said, pulling her skirt away from her heels before getting up. "She's busy. Come on and help, Fran."

Can this be? Fran thought, as she helped drape her

former tormentor. He's not frightening at all. *He's frightened.* She had never stood this close to him before.

Finished, Andrew mumbled, "Thanks," and took up a position across the hall, an aloof distance from Harold.

More groups disappeared. The plays were moving along.

Veronica pulled at her wig and yanked the hat farther down on her head. "What are you guys going to do next week?" she asked Fran and Nancy.

"Next week?" Fran's thoughts hadn't gone beyond tonight.

"How about going on a bicycle hike? We could take a picnic lunch."

"Fun!" Nancy said. "When?"

"Monday, Tuesday. Doesn't matter. Hey, is my make-up smeared? Never mind, let's get up there, we're next!"

The *Whistler's Song* group was getting ready to enter the stage door.

The *Go, Go Ghost* cast straggled down the hall, which was suddenly empty and quiet. Too scared to talk, they clustered around the stage entrance. Now Andrew and Harold, nervous eyes showing from behind the holes in the sheets, stayed close together for comfort.

Roxie quietly opened the stage door and slipped out. "Everyone all set? You look just fine." Her eyes lit on Veronica. "And you . . . well, you even scare me!" She grinned and rolled her eyes. Everyone laughed. "We've got a good audience out there, but," she added grimly, "a very noisy one. So project!"

Applause sounded from the auditorium. "Okay, get ready. Let the people out and then set your stage. Fast!"

"Ohhhh." Nancy and Fran gripped each other's arms. This was terrible. Fran was shaking all over and she could feel beads of perspiration rolling down her back.

She stumbled forward into the offstage darkness and pulled her sleeping bag from under a table. It was exactly where she had left it. Her fingers were trembling so badly she knew she could never undo the bag, feel around for a spider, and get it tied back in time.

"Places . . . lights!" Roxie called.

The light boy in the cage flicked switches and the curtain boy pulled on the cord. Light flooded the stage and filtered into the wings.

"This is it," someone whispered.

Rita gave a final pat to her hair and entered, followed by Sally and the other girls.

"See, it's just an old house."

"Yes, just an old haunted house. There's nothing to be afraid of, not really."

I hope not, Fran thought. Nancy, beside her, looked as stiff as a statue. A statue with lips clenched in her teeth. Where was Debbie sitting? Fran wondered. Down front? Would she be able to see her? If she saw Debbie she might not be able to concentrate. But she mustn't let her mind wander like this. She had to listen for her cue . . . *there it was!*

Like a windup toy, she entered the stage. Her voice, coming out with the familiar words, sounded like someone else's voice.

Fran moved, she talked, and suddenly, when the audience laughed at a funny line from Doreen, she felt herself not relaxing, exactly, but moving along with the play, stirred and excited. Why, this is what acting is, she thought. The audience is part of it!

Finally, alone on the stage with Nancy, she was able to transfer the fear she had felt into the part she was playing. *"I'm afraid,"* she said. *"A little."* But now it was the character who was afraid, not Fran herself.

The fear returned when it was time to get into the

sleeping bag. She tried to relax, but her legs felt stiff when she edged inside. Down, down, she moved. Her toes touched bottom. Nothing. Thank goodness. The worst was over.

"*What's that?*" came Nancy's line. "*I thought I heard something.*"

"*Me, too,*" Fran replied. But as she said it there was no loud moan. The awful thought struck her: the boys had missed their cue!

Nancy's back was toward the entrance the boys were supposed to come out of. Her face got a panicky look as she, too, realized the boys were not entering. She didn't know what was happening.

Fran could see. Just off stage two white figures were scuffling, paying no attention to the play.

"I . . . I . . . thought I heard a noise," Fran said "I . . . guess it's just my imagination."

Nancy stared at her, open-mouthed. These were new lines.

"Let's try to go to sleep," Fran fumbled. "Everything . . . will be all right." Now Nancy saw what was happening off stage. She looked at Fran, panic-stricken. "Lie down and go to sleep," Fran said.

Nancy continued to stare at her.

"There aren't any ghosts!" Fran shouted. The boys

185

heard. One gave the other a final punch and they stumbled onto the stage.

"I'll get you for this," Harold threatened.

Nancy screamed. That, at least, fit into the play.

"You won't get me!" Fran shouted, as though Harold had threatened her.

"Oh, no?" There was a wild chase, with shrieks and near-falls, which weren't in the script. Andrew's voice finally came through with a right line. They got back on the track.

In a few minutes, the girls made their exit. Fran and Nancy clung to each other in the wings, hardly able to catch their breath, while Veronica cackled and carried on in a way that had every child in the audience screeching.

Then it was time for Fran and Nancy to reenter the scene . . . and suddenly the play was over.

The curtains closed. The stage lights came on.

"Eee! We were just terrible, weren't we awful?" Rita trilled as Roxie came in, smiling broadly.

"You were all great," she exclaimed, "just wonderful! I . . . uh . . . must say, it was a different play in some ways. But it turned out fine." She gave Fran a special smile. "You did a good job there," she said.

Harold and Andrew struggled out of their sheets, which were dusty and torn.

"What happened to you two?" Roxie asked.

Andrew gave Harold a sideways look and grinned. "Nothing much. Just clowning around."

"In character to the end," Roxie observed. "Well, gang, it's good-bye now. I may see you next summer. If I get my health back." She grinned. "Take home your belongings because the school will be locked up next week." She left, followed by Rita, Sally, Claire, and the other club girls.

"Just a minute." Veronica took hold of Andrew's sleeve as he was about to leave. "What really happened back there?"

"Oh, this friend of mine here stuck a KICK ME sign on my back just before we were supposed to go on. Well, I wasn't about to leave it there and have everyone laugh."

"You really had to do that, didn't you?" Veronica said, glaring at Harold.

"Aw," Andrew said. "It doesn't really matter. It was just a joke. Wasn't it, pal?" He gave Harold a big slap on the back. He looked relieved and happy now that the play was over. "Come on, let's go."

"You ought to thank Fran for saving the play for you," Veronica said. "If she hadn't made up those lines you really would have looked silly."

"It's all right," Fran mumbled, embarrassed.

"Oh, well. Thanks." Andrew walked to the door. He turned. "Thanks a lot . . . Frantsy!"

"Don't call me — " But what was the use? Andrew was his same old self.

"Wait for me, Andrew," Harold called. He twisted his sheet over his arm and hurried after his friend. A big sign on his back said, KICK ME.

"I guess I'd better scram too," Veronica said. "My folks are waiting." She picked up her lantern. "Fran, how come you were able to make up those lines?"

Fran smiled. "I just pretended I was you."

"See you next week," Veronica said, ducking her head in pleasure. "On the bicycle hike. Bring Debbie what's-her-name too, if you want to."

"Oh, really? You wouldn't mind?"

"Now, why should I? The more the merrier. Right, Nancy?"

"Right!" Nancy said, glowing.

Fran took a final look around the empty stage. The cast was gone. The audience was gone. The play was over. And summer was almost over too.

I wish things could stay just as they are right now, Fran thought. But she had started out the summer with that same wish. If it had come about, she would not have gone to drama class nor made two such good friends.

Why, it isn't finished after all, she thought. The play is over, but new ones will begin.

And summer wasn't over, either. There were things to do and fun to be had. Fran ran from the stage and down the hall. She could hardly wait for another new beginning.

About the Author
At her kids' urging, Stella Pevsner began writing
books for children and young adults. Before that,
she worked as the publicity director for a large
cosmetics company, and as a copywriter for a
Chicago advertising agency. Mrs. Pevsner lives
in Palatine, Illinois, with her husband, two sons,
and two daughters.